DAY OF THE
MINOTAUR

D1638129

DAY OF THE MINOTAUR

THOMAS BURNETT SWANN

WILDSIDE PRESS

TO AUNT LITTLELY,
BELOVED

Copyright © 1966 by Thomas Burnett Swann

Published by Wildside Press LLC.
www.wildsidebooks.com

PREFACE

In 1952, when the young cryptographer, Michael Ventris, announced his partial decipherment of the clay tablets found in the ruins of Knossos, archaeologists, linguists, and laymen greeted his announcement with enthusiasm and expectation. Since the excavations of Sir Arthur Evans at the turn of the century, the island of the fabulous Sea Kings had piqued the imagination with its snake-goddesses and bull games, labyrinths and man-killing Minotaurs. But instead of a Cretan Iliad, the tablets revealed a commonplace inventory of palace furniture and foodstuffs, with occasional names of a town, a god, or a goddess. In a word, they confirmed the already accepted facts that the ancient Cretans had lived comfortably, worshiped conscientiously, and kept elaborate records. Those who had hoped for an epic, a tragedy, or a history—in short, for a work of literature to rival the Cretan achievements in architecture and fresco painting—were severely disappointed.

In 1960, however, an American expedition from Florida Midland University excavated a cave on the southern coast of Crete near the ancient town of Phaestus and discovered a long scroll of papyrus, sealed in a copper chest from the depredations of thieves and weather. I myself commanded that expedition and wrote the article which announced our find to the public. At the time of my article, we had barely begun to decipher the scroll, which I prematurely announced to be the world's earliest novel, the fanciful story of a war between men and monsters. But as we progressed with our decipherment, we marveled at the accurate historical framework, the detailed descriptions of flora and fauna, the painstaking fidelity to fact in costume and custom. We began to ask ourselves: Were we dealing, after all, with a novel, a fabrication, a fantasy? Then, last year, in the same cave, one of my colleagues discovered an intaglio seal ring of lapis lazuli which depicted a field of crocuses, a blue monkey, and a young girl of grave and delicate beauty. The discovery gave us pause: The identical ring had been described in the scroll, and its faithfully-rendered subjects, the monkey and the girl, were both participants in the so-called War of the Beasts.

My colleagues and I are scholars, objective and factual—the least romantic of men. We do not make extravagant claims. We do not suggest, however, that our manuscript, instead of the world's first novel, is one of its first histories, an authentic record of several months in the late Minoan Period soon after the year 1500 B.C., when the forests of Crete were luxuriant with oak and cedars and ruled by a race who called themselves the Beasts. We realize that the consequences of such a suggestion are breathtaking and may, in time, necessitate a complete reexamination of classical mythology, since many of our so-called 'myths' may in fact be sober history. What is more, folklorists may find in the scroll the prototype for a famous fairy tale long believed to have originated in the Middle Ages. Now, with considerable doubts and a rare, unscholarly excitement, we present to you the first English text of the manuscript which we have designated *Day of the Minotaur*. Wherever possible, proper names have been modernized for the convenience of the layman.

T.I. Montasque, Ph.D., Sc.D., L.L.D.
Florida Midland University,

July 29, 1964.

CHAPTER I
THE WOODEN WINGS

My history belongs to the princess Thea, niece of the great king Minos, and to her brother Icarus, named for the ill-fated son of Daedalus who drowned in the sea when his glider lost its wings. I, the author, am a poet and craftsman and not a historian, but at least I have studied the histories of Egypt and I will try to imitate their terse, objective style. You must forgive me, however, if now and then I digress and lose myself in the glittering adjectives which come so readily to my race. We have always been rustic poets, and I, the last of the line, retain an ear for the well-turned phrase, the elegant (yes, even the flowery) epithet.

Thea and Icarus were the only children of the Cretan prince, Aeacus, brother to Minos. As a young warrior, Aeacus had led a punitive expedition against a band of pirates who had raided the coast and taken refuge in the great forests of the interior. For three years no one heard of him. Returning at last to Knossos, he brought with him, instead of captured pirates, two small children. His own, he told the court. By whom? By a lady he had met on his wanderings. And where had he wandered? Through the Country of the Beasts, a forest of cypress and cedar shut from the rest of the island by the tall limestone ridges which humped from the range of Ida. Cynics concluded that Thea and Icarus were the offspring of a peasant; romanticists questioned if a mere peasant could have given birth to children as strange as they were beautiful, with neatly pointed ears and hair whose luminous brown held intimations of green. Thea took pains to hide her ears behind a cluster of curls, but she could not hide the color of her hair. Icarus, on the other hand, displayed his ears with a mixture of shyness and pride; he allowed no wisp of hair to cover their tips, though his head was a small meadow of green-glinting curls.

The children grew up in a troubled court. The power of the island kingdom had become a thin crescent of its ancient fullness. Gargantuan earthquakes had damaged the many-palaced cities. The famous fleet, scattered by tidal waves, had fallen into disrepair or come to be manned by mercenaries from Egypt. The bronze robot Tabs, guardian of the coast, lay rusting beside the great Green Sea, and no one remembered how to repair him. As the brother of Minos, Aeacus spent most of his time in the royal palace at Knossos, and after Minos' death he assumed the throne. A wise if somewhat forbidding ruler, he correctly guessed that the barbarous Achaeans, who lived in the rock-guilt citadels of Pylos, Tiryns, and Mycenae on the mainland to the north of Crete, were building ships to attack his people. The Achaeans worshiped Zeus of the Lightning and Poseidon, the Thunderer, instead of the Great Mother; their greatest art was war; and their raids on the Cretan coast resembled small invasions, with a dozen eagleprowed ships descending on a town in the dead of night to steal gold and capture slaves.

Foreseeing the eventual fall of Knossos, Aeacus sent his children—Thea was ten at the time, Icarus nine—to his mansion called Vathypetro, ten miles south of Knossos, a small, fortified, and self-sufficient palace which included a kiln, an olive press, and a weaving shop. Poised on the roof in the arms of a catapult lay one of the gliders devised by the late scientist, Daedalus. In case of siege, Aeacus' servants had orders to place the children on the fish-like body and strike the bronze trigger which, releasing the catapult, would propel them to relative safety in the heart of the island.

Six years after her arrival in Vathypetro, when invasion had become a certainty instead of a possibility, and the great palace at Mallia had fallen to pirates, Thea was picking crocuses in the North Court. The bright yellow flowers, known to poets as the cloth-of-gold, covered the earth like a rippling fleece, except where a single date-palm broke the flowers with its bending trunk and clustered, succulent fruit. She could hear, in the next court, the sounds of the olive-press, a granite boulder crushing the black kernels, the mush being poured into sacks and pressed under wooden levers weighted with stones. But the workers, the old and the very young who had not been called to the army defending Knossos, did not sound joyful; they did not sing their usual praises to the Great Mother. For want of sufficient pickers, the fruit had been left too long on the trees and its oil was crude and strong.

She wore a lavender kilt and a blouse embroidered at the neck with beads of amethyst. Though a young woman of sixteen, with shapely, swelling breasts, she did not like the open bodices worn by the ladies of the court. Five brown-green curls, artfully arranged by the handmaiden Myrrha, poised over her forehead, and three additional curls concealed each ear like grapevines hiding a trellis. Fresh and flower-like she looked, with the careful cultivation of a garden in a palace courtyard, rather than the wildness of a meadow or a forest; soft as the petals of a crocus, slender as the stem of a tall Egyptian lotus. But the green-flecked brown of her hair and the bronze of her skin resembled no flower in any earthly garden. Perhaps in the Lower World, where the Griffin Judge presides on his onyx throne, there are gardens with flowers like Thea.

And yet she was more than merely decorative. A firmness tempered her fragility. Like the purple murex, she looked as if she had come from the sea, fragrant and cleansed, with the shell's own hue in her eyes and its hard strength in her limbs. A sandal can crush a flower but not a murex.

She was picking the crocuses for her father, who, she hoped, was coming from Knossos to visit her. She saw him reflected in the pool of her mind: Aeacus the warrior-king. Tall for a Cretan, with broad shoulders tapering to a narrow waist, he looked like a young man until you saw the lines around his eyes, running like rivulets into his battle-scars: the v-shaped mark of an arrow, the cleft of a battle-ax. She needed his strength to hush her fears of an invasion, she needed his wisdom to help her manage Icarus, who sometimes acted as if he were five instead of fifteen and liked to vanish from the palace on mysterious journeys which he called his 'snakings.'

A blue monkey scampered out of the tree, snatched a crocus, and tossed it into the wicker basket at her feet. She laughed and caught him in her hands. Though a maiden of marriageable years, she did not resent the fact that for friends she had only a monkey, a handmaiden, and a lovable but ex-asperating brother; that instead of bull games and tumblers and moonlit dances beside the Kairatos River, she had for amusement a distaff to wind with flax and linen robes to dye. Escaping from her hands, the monkey, whose name was Glaucus, snatched her basket and carried it up the trunk of the palm. In the top of the tree, he dislodged a swarm of bees and waved the basket to advertise his theft.

She shook her fist as if she were very angry; she shook the tree and roared like an angry lion. It was part of their game. She remained, however, Thea; she did not feel remotely leo-nine. When Icarus turned himself into a bear, he growled, he stalked, he actually hungered after honey, berries, and fish. But even as a small child, the practical Thea had not liked to pretend herself into other shapes. "But why should I pretend to be a dolphin?" she had once asked a playmate. "I'm Thea." It was neither smugness nor lack of imagination, but a kind of unspoken acceptance, a quiet gratitude for the gifts of the Great Mother.

Always in the past, the monkey had dropped the basket at her feet and she, happily subsiding from lion into maiden, had rewarded him with a date or a honey cake. Today, however, she sank to the ground and, hunched among the flowers as if she had fallen from a tree, began to cry. It was not part of their game. She had heard the talk of the servants, their whispers when she approached, had seen the strain in her father's face the last time he came from Knossos. Against the unnatural pallor of his skin, his scars had glowed like open wounds. If my father comes, she thought, I will not let him return to Knossos. I will keep him safe with us in Vathypetro. If he comes.

The monkey descended the trunk, lifted the basket into her lap, and chattering amiably put his arm around her neck. She looked at him with surprise. Even at sixteen she was used to comforting instead of being comforted. Quickly she dried her eyes on a handkerchief of blue linen, with flying fish cavorting about its edges, and returned to picking.

"These are for my father," she said to Glaucus, "Do you suppose he will like them?" But she was not really thinking about the flowers. She was thinking about invasion. "If the walls are breached," her father had said, "you will go with Icarus to the Winged Fish. Myrrha will strap you to the board which is shaped like a mullet, and Icarus will hold to your back. Once in the air, you can shift your weight and help to change direction, climb or dip. Head for the mountains. Whatever you do, try not to land in the Country of the Beasts." He paused. He had spoken an ominous name, the part of the island where he had met their mother. It was hard to tell if he spoke with fear or with anguished longing for something which he had lost and did not want his children to find and also lose. "Pass over the forest before you land. By leaning heavily forward, you can bring the craft down. There are friendly villagers who will give you shelter."

She looked above the roofline of the mansion. To the north, Mount Juktas reared the gentle crags which, viewed from the sea, resembled the features of a sleeping god and barred the way to Knossos. Achaean invaders would come from the sea and around the mountain. To the west lay the hills, terraced with olive trees and vineyards, which climbed gradually into the Range of Ida and the Country of the Beasts, the forest which no one mentioned without a shudder, much less entered; the haunt, it was said by the cook, the gatekeeper, and the gardener, of the Minotaur, the Bull That Walks Like a Man. "Try not to land in the Country of the Beasts." She would not forget her father's warning.

Myrrha, the handmaiden exploded into the garden. At the same instant, Thea heard sounds beyond the walls. Marching feet, the clank of armor, the voices of men who march with such confidence that they want the whole countryside to hear their coming.

"Achaeans," Myrrha gasped. "We must go to the glider." She was black of skin, a Libyan born into slavery among the Cretans, and fearful of everything: monkeys, snakes, bats, mice, strangers, and as for the Achaeans—well, they were giants who boiled their captives in olive oil and ate them to the last finger. Thea did not know her age; it was doubtful whether Myrrha knew. Fifty? Sixty? But her face was as smooth as a girl's until, as now, it fell into wrinkled terror and her eyes seemed ready to burst from her head like overripe figs.

Myrrha seized her hand as if to comfort the girl, but it was Thea who imparted the strength and soothed the woman's fears. "The walls are strong. We may not need the glider." But privately she thought: The Achaeans come from the sea and from Knossos. There has been a battle; perhaps my father is dead.

She sprang up the stairs to the roof and surveyed the olive grove between the house and Mount Juktas. The green-silver limbs of the trees, some of them laden with fruit, glinted like the wings of dragonflies in the morning sun. But much of the glitter did not belong to the trees. Warriors, perhaps a hundred, advanced through the grove. Armored in leathern tunics, bronze cuirasses and crested helmets, with shields of bull's hide, they carried swords and spears, and their beards looked so coarse and pointed that they too might have been weapons. Sharp men, bristling men; yellow-bearded killers. Happily, the walled house was built to withstand a siege. The gate was hewn from cedar, and men in the flanking towers could harass attackers with relative impunity.

But the towers, it appeared, were no longer manned. The slaves and servants had begun to desert the house and trail down the road of cobblestones which led to the olive grove. They were laden with bribes for the conquerors—amphorae of wine, yellow cheeses on platters of beaten gold, wicker baskets heaped with linen and wool. Thea's impulse was to hurry after them and order them back by name: Thisbe, who had woven her kilt, Sarpedan, the porter, who called her "Green Curls," Androgeus… Surely they would listen, they who had seemed to love her and whom she had loved? No, there was not time. There was only time in which to find Icarus.

She ran along corridors with walls of porous ashlars and roofs supported by red, swelling columns like turned trees. Her sandals clattered on the gray ironstone tiles. She ran until she came to the Room of the Snake. The room was empty except for a low, three-legged table with four grooves which met in the middle and held a small cup, its rim on a level with the surface of the table. The snake's table. The grooves were to rest his body, the cup to hold his food. But the snake Perdix, protector of the mansion and, in the view of Icarus and the servants, a reincarnated ancestor, was not to be found on his table, not in his sleeping quarters, a terra cotta tube with cups attached to its ends. He lay in her brother's hand.

With utmost leisure, Icarus ambled toward her: a boy of fifteen, chunky rather than plump, with a large head and a tumult of hair and enormous violet eyes which managed to look innocent even when he was hiding Perdix in Myrrha's loom or telling Thea that she had just swallowed a poisonous mushroom. He never hurried unless he was leaving the house.

Thea embraced him with sisterly ardor. He submitted with resignation and without disturbing his snake. His sister was the only female he would allow to embrace him. Even as a small boy, he had spurned the arms of Myrrha and various ladies of the court at Knossos. Under normal circumstances— had he remained at court, for example—he could hardly have remained a virgin to the age of fifteen. He might be married;

certainly he would be betrothed. For the last five years, however, most of his playmates had been animals instead of boys and girls. The birth of a lamb, the mating of bull and cow: these were the familiar and hardly shocking facts of life to him. But he strenuously resisted the knowledge that men and women propagated in the same fashion.

"Perdix is ill," he explained. "I'm feeding him dittany leaves. They're good for cows in labor. Why not snakes with indigestion?"

"The Achaeans have come." She spoke the words in quick, breathless gasps. "Outside the palace. We must go to the glider." Myrrha by now had overtaken them.

His eyes widened but not with fear. "I will stay and fight them. You and Myrrha go."

She heard scuffling in the outer chambers, the shouts of Cretans, the oaths of Achaeans: "Poseidon!" "Athene!" A few of the servants, it appeared, had chosen to fight. A man screamed, the scream became a groan. Never had she heard such a sound except when her cat, Rhadamanthus, had been crushed by the stone wheel of a farmer's cart.

She fought back the nausea which clawed at her throat. "There are too many to fight."

"I will bring Perdix," he said. That flatness of his statement allowed no argument. A remarkable bond united the boy and his snake. For three years Icarus had squeezed and dropped him without arousing his wrath. The boy insisted that Perdix was the avatar of his great-great-uncle who had once sailed around the vast continent of Libya and returned with six pythons and a male gorilla.

"Yes. He will bring us luck."

And the blue monkey, Glaucus? Why had she not remembered to bring him from the garden? His little weight would not have slowed their flight.

They climbed the last stairs and burst into sunlight like breathless divers from the bottom of the sea. Raised on the catapult such as besiegers use to storm a city, the glider poised like a monster from the Misty Isles. Its wings were those of an albatross, with a framework of peeled willow rods covered by tough canvas; its wooden body was that of a fish with round, painted eyes and upturned tail. When the trigger of the catapult was struck with a hammer, two twisted skeins, made from the sinews of a sheep, would start to unwind and propel the craft upward along a trough at a 45-degree angle and into the air. There was room for two passengers, one on top of the other.

Myrrha was stooped with terror. She had started to mumble an incantation in her native tongue, a plea, no doubt, to the gods of the jungle.

"You and Icarus go," said Thea, touching the woman's shoulder. "I will strike the trigger."

But Myrrha shook her head and the terror ebbed from her face. She lifted the girl in her arms (for Cretans were little people, and Thea, although she had reached her full height, was less than five feet tall) and strapped her to the glider, securing leather straps to her arms and ankles. With a single, larger strap, she fastened Icarus to Thea's back.

"Hold to your sister," she ordered with unaccustomed authority. "The strap may break."

"How can I hold my snake at the same time?"

She took the snake, of which she was mortally afraid, and settled him in the pouch at the front of Icarus's loincloth. "He will think it's his tube," she reassured the boy.

They did not hear the arrow. Myrrha was speaking to Icarus; then, without a scream, she settled onto the roof and almost deliberately seemed to stretch her limbs in an attitude of sleep. The arrow was very small and nearly hidden in the folds of her robe. With its feathered tail, it looked like a bird gathered to her breast.

Icarus freed their straps and slid with Thea onto the roof. He knelt beside his nurse and kissed her cheek for the first and last time. She lay with her usual expression of doubt and perplexity. Thea stifled a sob; there was no time for tears. She jerked Icarus to his feet. She herself would have to strike the trigger and send him to safety without her.

He saw her intention. "No," he protested. "I am a man. It is you who must go." She was always surprised when her brother issued commands; in his placid times, people forgot his stubbornness. He shoved her towards the glider.

She slapped him across the mouth. "Do you want us both to die?" she cried. "Now do as I say. Remember, you are not to land in the Country of the Beasts."

A giant had barred their path. An Achaean, though not the deadly bowman. The topmost rung of his ladder leaned against the edge of the roof. A bronze helmet, crested with peacock feathers, concealed his forehead, but she saw his blond eyebrows and beardless cheeks; he was very young. There was blood on his hands and on the sword which he raised above his head. She smelled the leather of his tunic as he strode toward her. With a speed which belied his great, clumsy-looking arms, he dropped the sword and locked both children in a fierce hug. They wriggled like netted tunnies and slid to the floor, gasping for breath—fish spilled on a beach.

He knelt beside them and brushed the curls from Thea's ears. She shuddered at the touch of his fingers.

He grinned, "Pointed ears," he said in the rich Achaean tongue which she had learned at court, a strangely musical language for a race of warriors. "You are not Cretan at all. I think you have come from the woods, and it's time you returned." His eyes were as blue as the feathers of a halcyon, the bird which nests on the sea and borrows its color from the waves; and a faint amber down had dusted his cheeks. She thought with a wave of tenderness: he is trying to raise a beard and resemble his bristling comrades. In spite of his size and strength, he seemed misplaced in armor.

He placed them on the glider and fastened their thongs. "You had better go. My friends are rough."

He struck the trigger with the hilt of his sword. She hoped that his friends would not be angry with him.

She could not breathe; her brother's body seemed a weight of bronze. Up, up, they shot; up into sunlight and lapis lazuli, where Daedalus had flown, and that other Icarus, for whom her brother was named, until he lost his wings and plunged into the sea like a stricken albatross.

She opened her eyes. The wind's invisible cobwebs had ceased to sting. She felt like a Dancer in the Games of the Bull, swimming the air above the deadly horns; or a dolphin, leaping a wave for the sheer joy of sun above him and sea below him, and air around him like a coolness of silk.

Then she saw their direction.

"Shift," she cried to Icarus. "We are heading for the coast!"

Silence.

"Icarus, listen to me. You mustn't be afraid. You must help me steer for the mountains!"

"Afraid?" he protested, "I wasn't afraid. I was thinking about birds. Now I know what it means to get a bird's-eye view!"

"Shift," they cried in unison abandoning themselves to the breathless joy of flight.

"SHIFT!"

Below them the captured palace twinkled its giant mosaic—the blue-black clay of the roofs, the red gypsum of the courtyards, punctuated by gardens and fountains and swelling toadstools of smoke which did not come from the hearth in the kitchen. Scarlet blades of flame began to probe among the mushrooming blacknesses. So, too, she thought, had burned the palace of Knossos. Capture, pillage, and burn: that is the way of Achaeans. And her father? She blanched to think of him among such flames.

Grief froze in her like water in a pool, and high among the clouds, time too seemed frozen, as if all the water clocks had turned to ice and the shadows on all the sundials were fixed to a certain hour. And yet they moved. Time and pain were frozen but not the earth, which changed below them from stone village linked by roads to hamlets linked by footpaths; from vineyards and olive groves to pastures scattered with thickets and shepherds' huts and undulating upwards, upwards toward the Mountains of Ida.

A peak surged toward them like an angry whale. "Shift!"

They skirted the snowcapped crags, and winds lashed them like spray from a wintry sea.

And then, cupped in the arms of the old, white-haired mountains, lay a green forest, its single egress a narrow strip of the south which faced toward the rich Messara Valley and the great city of Phaestus.

The Country of the Beasts.

They began to descend, gently but irrevocably, toward the forest. Cypresses, bronze in the afternoon sun; cedars as old as the time when the infant Zeus had been nursed in these very mountains; pines and firs, and lesser trees which they did not recognize, wafting a strange fragrance up to meet them, sweet and acid at once (myrrh? sandarac?): a green immensity of trees, with grassy glades and a stream of flawless malachite, and there, there—was it a town or only a natural clearing with stunted trees like houses and a ditch like a girdling moat? No man except their father was known to have entered the Country of the Beasts. Shepherds, following sheep, had skirted the southern boundary and seen among the shadows boys with hooves of goats, winged females with staring golden eyes, and yes, the Minotaur, the Bull That Walks Like a Man.

"Thea," whispered Icarus, a hushed eagerness in his voice. "Why don't we try to land in the forest?"

"No," she cried with sudden vehemence. "You know what Father said."

"But nothing happened to him. And he left our mother in there."

"Our mother is dead. Now shift."

She threw her weight to the left, but Icarus stared at the forest and did not move.

"Icarus!"

"Yes," he said quietly, "Yes, Thea."

The treetops, soft from a distance, bristled with gnarled fingers to puncture their wings; but together they managed to guide their craft beyond the forest, to a clearing of grass and yellow, early-blooming asphodels. They struck with such a thud that they broke their straps and tumbled onto the ground. The lily-like asphodels cushioned their fall.

"Thea, look!" whispered Icarus. "There is something watching us." She looked to the edge of the forest and saw the face.

"Her ears," said Icarus, forgetting to whisper. "They're just like ours!"

"No," said Thea quickly. "Hers are furry. Ours are merely pointed. And besides, she has—paws!"

The face eclipsed itself behind a tree. "We frightened her away," sighed Icarus.

"It was something else that frightened her." Achaeans. At least a score of them, issuing onto the meadow.

"We can follow the girl," cried Icarus.

"No," said Thea, "Better Achaeans than Beasts."

Chapter II

THE MINOTAUR

His helmet of boar's tusk glittered yellowly in the light from the clerestory windows. His bronze cuirass fell below his thighs; he removed his greaves, grunting with easeful release, and his huge, hairy legs resembled trees rising from the undergrowth of his rawhide boots. To Thea, he looked elderly; he must have been forty. He lifted the helmet from his sweat-matted hair and faced his young captives in the hall of a Cretan nobleman's captured mansion. Thea and Icarus awaited his judgment. His name was Ajax; his men had taken them beside their glider.

On the frescoed walls, blue monkeys played in a field of crocuses. Red-stained columns, swelling into bulbous capitals, supported the roof, and the alabaster floor was divided by strips of red stucco. A riot of color and movement, freedom and playfulness: unutterably foreign to the hard-bitten conquerors with their shields and swords. They seemed to sense their unwelcome; they stood gingerly on foam-white alabaster and stared at the painted walls as if they expected the monkeys to drown them with derisive chattering.

She sought her brother's hand and felt his returning pressure. A warmth of tenderness, like the current from a glowing brazier, enveloped her; then a chill of remorse, as if the brazier had been extinguished. It was she who had caused their capture, preferring known barbarians to unknown Beasts.

Ajax sighed and slumped in a chair with a back of carved griffins. To such a man, thought Thea, fighting is not an art but a livelihood; he is not a hero but a strong, stupid, reasonably brave animal who fights because he is too lazy to plant crops or sail a ship.

A small, wedge-shaped wound glowed in his forehead. "You Cretans," he said, pointing to the wound. "For such little creatures you have sharp claws. The lady of the house gave me this." He laughed. "She was suitably punished." He motioned Thea and Icarus to approach his chair.

Icarus stepped in front of his sister. "You are not to harm her."

"Harm her? Not if she pleases me," Ajax grunted without rancor, disclosing a gap in place of his middle teeth. His voice was high and thin; it squeaked from his hulking body like a kitten's mew from a lion. But he gestured and flared his nostrils as if he were Zeus, the sky-god. "My men saw your ship come down. You almost landed in the Country of the Beasts."

"I wish we had," said Icarus.

"Do you?" Ajax laughed. "You'd like for the Minotaur to get your sister? He takes his pleasure with girls and then he eats their brothers. A Cretan boy like you would make one good bite—except for your head. That might stick in his throat."

"Does he live in the woods where we landed?" asked Icarus, totally uncowed.

A young warrior, both of whose ears had been sliced from his head as neatly as mushrooms from a log, anticipated his leader. "His lair is a cave a little to the west. The people hereabouts offer him lambs and calves so he won't come out and eat their children. When we took this house, they called his curse down on us."

Ajax silenced the speaker with an oath. "To Hades with Cretan curses! They're no more potent than Cretan goddesses. Now take these children to the Room of the Dolphins and see that the girl has the means to bathe and change."

She felt his eyes on her wind-disheveled hair and instinctively reached a hand to rearrange her curls.

"Pointed ears," he remarked, apparently noticing for the first time. "And your brother as well. Are you from the forest?"

Angrily Thea restored her curls, "We are Cretans, not Beasts. If I were a Beast, my ears would be tipped with fur."

"Well then, my girl with the furless ears, I will come to see you within the hour. See that you robe yourself as becomes a woman and not a child. I have no wish to be reminded of my daughter."

The Room of the Dolphins was small, like most of the rooms in the sprawling palaces of Crete. It was intimate and gaily decorated, with terracotta lamps, as yet unlit, perched like pigeons in wall-niches; folding chairs of fragrant citrus wood; and a raised stone platform billowing cushions of goose feather. On one end, it opened between two columns into a light well with a black wooden pillar to honor the Great Mother; on the other, into a bathroom with a sunken floor and a small clay bathtub around whose sides an impudent painted mouse pursued a startled cat. In the center of the room stood an open chest whose contents were strewn on the floor like a treasure cast from the sea: golden pendants aswarm with amber bees, sandals of blue kidskin, gowns of wool, leather, and linen with wide, flaring skirts. The earless Xanthus pointed to the dresses, nodded to Thea, and paused with eager expectancy, hoping no doubt to watch her disrobe in front of him. Because they display their breasts, the ladies of Crete are sometimes thought to be shameless.

She could not be cross with the man in spite of his impudence. There was something pathetic about his missing ears; without them, his head looked undressed. She smiled tolerantly and pushed him toward the door. The merest touch of her hand impelled him to motion, and he moved before her like a ship before a breeze.

Leaving Icarus to admire the fresco of dolphins, she climbed in the tub and turned a frog-shaped spigot to immerse her body with hot, steaming water. In the larger mansions, rain was trapped on the roof, heated by a brazier, and carried to the bathrooms through pipes of terracotta. Cretan plumbing was admired even in Egypt. She drowsed and forgot to lament the past or dread the future; anxieties flowed from her body along with dust and sweat and the stains of grass and flowers. A sound awoke her, a lapping of water.

"Thirsty," said Icarus. He had knelt by the tub to offer Perdix a drink, and the snake's forked tongue was narrowly missing her arm.

She shrank to the rear of the tub. She was not embarrassed in front of her brother—often they had bathed or swum to-gether without clothes—but she did not wish to be bitten by her great-great uncle. Though none of the snakes of Crete were poisonous, some like Perdix possessed sharp fangs.

"Does he have to drink now?" she cried.

"He likes it hot, you know. It reminds him of underground springs." When the snake had drunk his fill, Icarus raised him from the water and held him as casually as one might hold a piece of rope or a few links of chain. "I chose a gown for you," he continued. "Hurry up and dress before the water gets cold. Perdix and I want to bath too."

Icarus and Perdix possessed the vacated tub, which lacked a drain and would have to be emptied by Ajax's attendants before it could be refilled. While Icarus splashed in the tub and complained about slow sisters who let the water cool, Thea examined the gown he had chosen for her. It was very bold. The crimson skirt was embroiderd with golden heads of gorgons, the puffed sleeves with matching serpents. The bodice was open to reveal the breasts. She smiled at Icarus' taste and chose a more decorous gown which covered her breasts with a thin, diaphanous gauze. Sleeves of saffron fell to her elbows, and the skirt, supported by hoops, flared like an amethyst bell.

"He is going to be disappointed," said Icarus, entering the room. "He wanted you to dress 'as becomes a woman.'"

"Haven't I?"

"You know very well what he meant. He wanted to see your breasts. Myrrha always said they were like melons, and if they kept on growing they would soon be pumpkins. I expect he feels like gardening."

"He can see enough of them now."

"I know but you've diminished them. Perhaps you could paint your nipples with carmine."

"Do you want me to look like a Moabite temple girl?" she protested, though nipples were also painted in worldly Knosses.

"It can't hurt to pacify him," said Icarus realistically.

She thought with a start: He does not suspect what Ajax really wants of me. He still believes that a woman pleases a man only by showing her breasts and perhaps giving him a kiss.

"You see," he went on, "if he likes your dress, he may not make you kiss him."

"If he likes my dress, he will make me kiss him."

Icarus looked surprised. "But that seems greedy. Must he get everything the first night?"

"Achaeans are greedy men. That's why they've come to Crete."

"Of course," he admitted. "You are right then to veil your breasts." From the contents of the chest he selected a pendant of amber and placed it protectively around her neck. "This," he said, "will diminish them even more."

She arranged her curls with the help of copper pins, their heads like tiny owls; reddened her cheeks with ochre; and darkened her eyes with kohl. She was not vain; she was fastidious. She did not dress to make herself beautiful, but to perform an indispensable ritual by which she emphasized the degree and discipline of her ancient civilization. The application of cosmetics was an affirmation of order in a world which, because of earthquakes and Achaeans, threatened to grow disorderly to the point of chaos.

Hardly had she finished her toilet when Xanthus invaded the room with a swollen platter of grapes, figs and pomegranates, withdrew, and returned with a copper flagon of wine and two cups, which he placed on a three-legged table of stone. Then, with the help of coals from a portable brazier, he lit the flaxen wicks of the clay lamps and went to fetch his master.

"Xanthus," said Ajax, entering the room with the leer of a man who is about to enjoy a woman and be envied by other men, "stand guard at the door with Zetes and don't disturb us." Withdrawing, Xanthus returned the leer, and Thea ceased to pity him for his severed ears.

"You will sleep in there," Ajax said to Icarus. He handed the boy a cushion and indicated the floor of the bathroom, beside the tub. "Your sister and I are going to dine."

"I'm not sleepy," said Icarus. "The evening is still youthful. However, I am hungry."

"Help yourself to the fruit, but eat it in the bathroom."

Icarus eyed the fruit without enthusiasm and eyed his sister as if he hoped for a sign. It was plain to see that Ajax had kisses in mind. What should they do?

But Thea could not help him. Fear had left her speechless. A disagreeable adventure threatened to become a disaster. Ajax could break her back with the fingers of one hand.

"You know," continued Icarus valiantly, "it's not the food I want so much as the conversation. My great-great uncle Perdix used to say: 'Good company is worth a broiled pheasant, a flagon of wine, and all the honey cakes you can get on a platter.'"

Thea recovered her speech. "Icarus would enjoy eating with us. You see, he hasn't known any warriors except his father. You could show him how to handle a dagger."

"Yes," said Icarus, reaching toward the dagger in Ajax's belt, a bronze blade with a crystal hilt. "It's the biggest I ever saw. Why, even a wild boar—"

Before he could finish his sentence, Ajax had swallowed him in his massive arms and swept him toward the door of the bathroom. There was something almost paternal about the scene. In the giant's embrace, the chunky Cretan looked like a small boy being carried to bed by an irate, but loving father. Thea remembered that Ajax had mentioned a daughter.

When Ajax returned, the door shutting behind him on its vertical wooden pivot, Thea had formed a plan. At the age of eleven in Knossos, before she had gone with Icarus to Vathypetro, she had learned to parry the advances of amorous boys; on sun-dappled Crete, young bodies ripened like succulent dates and love came with first adolescence.

Smiling, she motioned Ajax to a chair. "He's a lonely child," she said, gesturing toward the closed door behind which she did not doubt that Icarus had knelt to listen. "He misses a man's company. You see, our father was killed by pirates three years ago."

"Achaean?"

"Yes," she sighed. "They attacked the ship on which he was sailing to Zakros." It was not hard to invent a touching story. "Women have raised us. Not our mother, who died when Icarus was born, but servants and aunts. Always women. How we have missed a man." She offered him a cup of wine. He touched the brim to his lips, tasting gingerly, as if he suspected poison. She walked behind him and placed her hand on his forehead.

"You must let me bathe your wound." she said. "Pretend that I am your daughter. Before he was killed, I used to tend my father with soft unguents and comb his wind-tossed hair. Like you, he was a fighter and often hurt."

He seized her wrist with unpaternal roughness and drew her into his lap. "The skirt becomes you," he said, draining his cup in one continuous swallow. "But not the blouse," With a single and surprisingly deft movement for such a ponderous hand, he tore the gauze from her breasts. His body reeked of leather and sweat. He could not have bathed in weeks, possibly months; he had doffed his armor but he wore the same tunic which he had worn in battle (in several battles, she decided; it was stained with blood, dirt, and food). Furthermore, he was densely wooded with hair: his legs, his arms, even the tops of his sandaled feet. He reminded her of a large hirsute goat, and like a goat he seemed to her foolish rather than threatening. She had not yet learned that a strong fool is the most dangerous of men.

"You need more wine," she said, trying to disengage herself. Perhaps she could incapacitate him with drink. According to a universal proverb, variously claimed by Cretans, Egyptians, and Babylonians, drinking increases desire, but limits performance.

"Not wine. This—" He buried her mouth with a kiss which tasted of onions. She remembered that Achaean soldiers chewed them as they marched. She felt as if heavy masculine boots were trampling the delicate offerings—murex, coquina, starfish—in a seaside shrine to the Great Mother. It was not that she feared dishonor, like the god-fearing women of Israel, the faraway kingdom of shepherded patriarchs. As a Cretan girl, she was realistic enough to recognize that there was nothing dishonorable if he took her, a woman and a captive, against her will. It was his dirt she feared, his ugliness, his hairiness, his affront to her feminine pride (remember, the Cretans worship a goddess as their chief deity). It was the supreme disorder of being forced to do what seemed to her not a wicked but an ugly and demeaning thing.

His kiss grew more impassioned. She clenched her teeth to withstand his probing tongue. Loathing burned in her like a black, bitter fire of hemlock roots.

"I lost my snake," said a loud and determined voice from the door. Ajax leaped to his feet, and Thea embraced the hard but welcome coolness of the floor.

Rising to her knees, she watched the advance of the snake. He was neither large not poisonous but, flickering his forked tongue, he somehow managed to look as sinister as an asp from the deserts of Egypt. Ajax seized a stool and assumed the martial stance of a soldier defending a bridge against an army.

But Icarus intervened before they could meet. "You mustn't scare him," he said, restoring the snake to his pouch. "It makes him nervous, and then he bites."

"Guard!"

Xanthus appeared in the door beyond the light well. As usual, he looked expectant; perhaps he hoped for an orgy.

"Xanthus, you will take this brat and his snake into the bathroom and keep them there, if you have to drown them in the tub."

The door to the bathroom closed with abrupt finality.

"You Cretan girls," sneered Ajax. He came toward her, shaggy and menacing. 'You tease and mince and show your breasts, and then you say. "No, you hairy old barbarian, you shan't touch me!' Barbarians, are we? Well, we know what to do with a woman!"

"My father will kill you if you touch me." The words stabbed the air like little daggers of ice.

"Oh? He's back from Hades, is he? Indeed. I should fear a man who escapes Persephone!"

In spite of his golden beard, he seemed all darkness and evil, a black whirlwind of fire and rock. The smell of him bit her nostrils like volcanic ash. She knotted her fists in tiny impotence.

Then she remembered the pins in her hair.

* * * *

She watched their torch-bearing captors recede in the distance like fishing boats into the night and leave them to darkness that seemed to smother their senses like a shroud of black wool. The air was rank with the droppings of bats. Icarus clutched her hand, half in protection, half in fear. She too was afraid; much more than he, she guessed, since caves and cliffs and roaring rivers, all of the fierce faces of nature, had long been familiar to him from his roving near Vathypetro.

"Possibly," said Icarus without reproach, "if you had struck him somewhere else, he wouldn't have been so angry."

"Nowhere else would have stopped him."

"He certainly had to be stopped," agreed Icarus. "I heard him screaming at you. And all for a kiss."

It was hardly the time to tell him the facts which he had resisted from Myrrha. The cave, of course, belonged to the Minotaur.

She drew him close to her and felt his big head against her shoulder. "Forgive me," she said. "Forgive me, little brother."

"But I wanted to come to the Country of the Beasts," he reminded her, not yet frightened enough for a sentimental exchange of endearments. "Now we've come."

"You didn't want the Cave of the Minotaur."

"Perdix will bring us luck."

"Not against the Minotaurs. They are much too big."

"Maybe this one is out to dinner."

"I'm afraid he dines at home. Shhhh," said Thea. "I hear—"

They heard a padding of feet (or hooves?), and then a low, long-drawn wail which deepened and reverberated into the curdling bellow of an enraged bull. Nausea crept to her throat like the furry feet of a spider.

"Mother Goddess, he's coming!" groaned the boy.

"We must separate," said Thea. "Otherwise, he will get us both at once. We'll try to slip past him in the dark and meet at the mouth of the cave."

"Won't he be able to see us? This is his lair."

"He can't chase us both at once."

"Let him chase me first. If he's a slow eater, you may have a chance."

"He will make his own choice." She both expected and hoped to be chosen before her brother. If the Minotaur added the instincts of a man to those of a bull, he ought to prefer a girl to a boy.

She loosened Icarus' hand. His fingers lingered; he hugged her in a quick, impulsive embrace and darted ahead of her, moving from darkness to darkness, scraping his sandals on the floor of the cave. She started to call his name. No, she must not alert the Minotaur. She began to feel her way along the walls; their dampness oozed like blood between her fingers. Once, she stumbled and cut her knee on stalagmites, for she wore her kilt and not the bell-shaped skirt in which she greeted Ajax. A stench pervaded the air, rancid and sweet at the same time: putrescent flesh and dried blood. She stopped often to catch her breath; fear had drained her as if she had breasted a strong, outgoing tide and washed on the beach with driftwood and shells. Little by little, her eyes became used to the darkness and distinguished the pronged stalactites which hung from the roof like seaweed floating above a diver's head.

Why, she asked herself, do I fear the Minotaur more than Ajax and his killers? At Knossos, she had often attended the Games of the Bull; once, it is true, she had seen a boy impaled, but the bull had not been vicious.

The boy had tried to somersault over his back but landed on his horns. The bull had seemed surprised instead of murderous; he had lowered his horns to help the attendants remove the body.

Sounds, muffled and dim (Icarus' voice, perhaps?). Then, again, the long-drawn, chilling roar.

The bull that walks like man, that was the terror. Walks on two legs. Thinks with a man's cunning, hates with a man's calculated cruelty. A hybrid of man and beast, monstrous to the eye, monstrous of heart, and roaring with cold malevolence.

A yearning for Icarus hushed her fears. The tentative touch of his hand, restless to dart away like a plump woodmouse. The big head, not really big except for its wreath of hair, and the pointed ears which he did not allow the hair to conceal. His childish games and hardly childlike courage. She bit her tongue to keep from calling his name. She rounded a turn and looked up and up into the eyes of the Minotaur, and his red, matted hair.

* * * *

When I entered the cave, I was hungry as a bull. Once a week the farmers outside the forest bring me a skinned animal. Bellowing lustily to justify my reputation, I fetch the meat and take it home with me to cook in my garden. They call me the Minotaur, the Bull That Walks Like a Man. In spite of my seven feet, however, I am not a freak, but the last of an old and illustrious tribe who settled the island before the Cretans arrived from the East. Except for my pointed ears (which are common to all of the Beasts), my horns (which are short and almost hidden by hair), and my unobtrusive tail, I am far more human than bovine; though my generous red hair, which has never submitted to the civilizing teeth of a comb, is sometimes mistaken for a mane.

As I said, I came into the cave with a hearty appetite. I also came harassed by a trying day in my workshop. My lapidaries, the Telchines, had quarreled and bruised each other with chisels and overturned a vat of freshly fermented beer. My stomach rumbled with anticipation of the plump, neatly skinned lamb (perhaps two) which would soon be revolving on the spit in my arden.

Almost at once I heard noises. I stopped in my tracks. Had my dinner been brought to me unkilled, unskinned, and uncleaned? Intolerable! It looked as if I would have to prowl the countryside after dark and strike terror into the hearts of the shiftless peasants.

But no. The sounds were voices and not the ululations of animals. I stalked down the twisting corridors of what is called the Cave of the Minotaur but which might better be called his Pantry. I paused. I peered. I sniffed. Man-scent was strong in the air. A trap? Well, they were not likely to trap a Minotaur. I could see in the dark, and my nose was as keen as a bear's. I advanced warily but confidently hoof over hoof. I—

Crunch!

A rock struck my outstretched hoof. I roared with pain, hobbled on the other leg, and looked up to face my attacker, who was crouched on an overhanging ledge and readying another rock.

I saw a chunky boy of about fifteen, with a large and very engaging head, a thicket of greenish hair, and pointed ears. The ears, to say nothing of the hair, marked him as a Beast. At least, half of him. I liked both halves. He was the kind of boy that one would like to adopt as a brother. Help him to carve a bow from the branches of a cedar tree and spear fish with a sharpened willow-rod and, at the proper time, introduce him to the Dryad, Zoe, and her free-living friends, who could teach him about a boy's way with a wench.

"Come down from there," I cried. "What do you think you are, a blue monkey? I won't hurt you."

"Oh," he said, surprised. "You can talk, and in Cretan too."

"What did you expect me to do, moo or speak Hittite? As a matter of fact, your people learned their language from my people several hundred years ago."

"Till now I have only heard you bellow." He was already climbing down from his ledge.

I reached out and seized hold of him and, suddenly mischievous, delivered my heartiest bellow right in his face. He trembled, of course, but looked me straight in the eye.

"You shouldn't have come down so quickly," I chided. "I might have been luring you down to eat."

"But you said you wouldn't hurt me."

"Don't believe everything you're told. If I had been a Cyclops, I would have smiled and coaxed and stirred you in the pot!"

"What should I have done?"

"Argued a bit. Asked for proof of my good intentions. Found out what I meant to do with you."

"But you didn't eat me, and I saved time and questions. I want you to meet my sister."

My heart sank like a weight from a fisherman's net.

The sister of such a brother was certain to be a lady. Let me say at once: wenches have always liked me, but ladies shut their doors. I would frighten her, she would call me (or, being a lady, think me) uncouth and uncivilized. She would want me to comb my hair, shave my chest, and trim my tail. She would wince when I swore, glare if I tippled beer, and disapprove of my friends, Zoe, the Dryad, and Moschus, the Centaur.

"Oh," I said, "I don't think she will want to meet me."

"She will be delighted. She thought she was going to have to pleasure you."

We walked to meet her while Icarus told me about their adventures. The meeting was to change my life.

Chapter III

THE TRUNCATED TREE

Do you know the pottery called Kamares Ware? Thin as an eggshell, swirling with creatures of the sea: anemones, flying fish, and coiling octopi. You would think that the merest touch would crack the sides, and yet in a hundred years the same cup can still hold flowers of wine or honey. That was Thea. The littleness of her, the soft fragility, stirred me to tenderness. At the same time, I saw her strength. Her slender waist, slim as the trunk of a young palm tree, rose into powerful breasts like those of an Earth Mother; her tiny hands were clenched and raised like weapons.

Icarus ran ahead of me and took her hand. "Don't be afraid," he cried. "He wants to be our friend." He added, rather proudly: "Even though I bashed him with a rock."

I stood awkwardly, shifting my weight from hoof to hoof, and wondered what I could say to reassure her. "He's right," I blurted. "I want to be your friend, and you won't have to pleasure m-m-me." I stammered into silence. To mention pleasuring to a lady—well, it was just such tactless remarks, together with my physiognomy, which had branded me as a boor for most of my twenty-six years. I awaited the lifted eyebrow, the frigid smile, the stinging slap.

She took my hand—paw, I should say, since her small fingers could not encircle its girth. I returned the pressure as shyly as if I were holding a thrush's egg.

"Sir," she said, "we have come to your place without invitation. May we remain as grateful guests?"

"I don't live here," I cried with some vexation, "I have a comfortable house in the forest." Had she been the Dryad Zoe, words would have tripped from my tongue with the ease of fruit from an upturned cornucopia, and my own eloquence would have put me in mellow spirits. As it was, I was desperately frightened of her and trying to hide my fear with a show of petulance.

"May we then—" she began.

"Follow me," I growled, turned my back, and strode toward the mouth of the cave. When I did not hear them directly behind me, I paused and looked over my shoulder. They were limping and stumbling across the rough stalagmites. Thea had bruised her knee and Icarus had taken her hand. I went back to them, lifted her in my arms, and ordered Icarus to ascend my back.

"You don't mind carrying a snake too?" he asked.

"Snakes," I said, "are symbols of fertility and domesticity. They bring growth to the fields and fortune to the house. Besides that, they are somebody's ancestors."

"Great-great-uncles," said Icarus. He started to wave his arms and shout, "Giddyap!"

"With two riders, I am doing well to lope," I said. "If you want to gallop, I suggest you find a Centaur. Bend down now or you'll bump your head."

"Better than goose feathers," he mumbled, making a pillow out of my hair, and Thea lay in my arms as lightly as a sleeping child. It came to me with startling suddenness that I had gone to the cave in search of dinner and found a family. To a confirmed and somewhat dissolute bachelor like myself, the new responsibility was terrifying.

At the mouth of the cave, I set them down on the moss and caught my breath.

"What big trees," cried Icarus, looking at the forest which stretched around us like tall Egyptian obelisks. "Big enough to hold houses in their branches."

"Or in their trunks," I said. "That's where the Dryads live." There were cedars with clustered needles and small, erect cones; wide-spreading, many-acorned oaks with bark like the cracked, discarded skin of a snake; and cypresses, lithe and feminine, their leaves misting with sunlight.

"How sad they look," said Thea, pointing to the cypresses. "Like women. The women of all ages who have known the wrenchings of childbirth or the caged swallow which is unrequited love."

"And yet," I said, "they look as if they have borne these things proudly and willingly. It is courage you see as well as sadness."

"Of course," she agreed. "You must forgive me for sounding morbid. Ever since we lost our home, I have felt as if—as if sadness had fallen on me like a hunter's net!"

I understood her needs. She wanted a house to shut her from forests, Achaeans, and—who knows? Minotaurs. She wanted a warm hearth, a father and perhaps a husband (for she was ripe for marriage).

"Little princess," I said. "We will soon be safe in my house. There you will not feel lost."

She smiled at me with a sweetness older than Babylon, older than the pyramids at Gizeh which house the mummified bodies of Egyptian pharaohs. The sun of the late afternoon kindled her hair in a smoky radiance. Why do you fight the forest, I thought. The brown of your hair is the rich soil from which the barley grows; it is the trunk of a tree or the wing of a thrush. The green is the first tentative blade that reaches for sunlight; it is leaves and grass and the young grape. Brown and green. Earth's two colors. Why do you fear the forest?

Then, through the blue smoke of time, I remembered my own boyhood. In the branches of a tree, I saw a small girl weeping, and a small boy who laughed and waved his pink fist, and the Dryad, their mother, who leaned to the sunlight and combed her hair. And him, not a Beast, but a man.

To reach my house we followed a secret path whose signs were a woodpecker's nest and a mound of yellow hill-ants, a stone in the shape of a fist, and a blackened stump. Sometimes we walked in a darkness of tangled limbs which withheld the sun except for a few golden icicles; in a closeness of air which dampened and weighted us as if we were walking the bottom of the sea. High in the trees, blue monkeys flickered like fish, and only their cries reminded us that we walked in a forest of trees instead of coral and holothurians. Thea waved to them gaily and coaxed their leader to sit on her shoulder, draping his tail like a necklace around her throat.

"I had one in Vathypetro." She smiled. "They don't seem part of the forest. They are tame like Egyptian cats."

"Too tame for their own good," I said. "Sometimes they get themselves eaten by bears."

"Look," cried Icarus suddenly. "A sea of flowers and a little brown fort in the middle."

"Yellow gagea," I said, adding modestly, "the fort is my house."

The house had once been a mountainous oak, broad as the Ring of the Bulls at Knossos, but thanks to a bolt of lightning, only the trunk remained to a height of twenty feet, like the walls of a palisade with a walkway and narrow embrasures near the top in case of a siege. I went to the door and rang the sheep's bell which hung above the lintel. Behind the red-grained oak I heard the quick pattering steps of a Telchin as he came to raise the bolt. In the forest, it was always necessary to lock one's door. According to an old proverb, "Where locks are not, the Thriae are." The shy Telchin did not wait to greet us. He and his race are frightened of strangers, though among themselves they boast and wench and fight at the drop of a toadstool.

I had hollowed the trunk of my tree to encompass a garden, which held a folding chair of citrus wood, a large reed parasol like those of the Cretan ladies when they walk by the sea, a clay oven for bread and honey cakes, a grill for roasting meat, and a fountain of hot spring water which served as my bath and also to wash my dishes. Around the fountain grew pumpkins, squashes, lentils, a grapevine hugging a trellis, and a fig tree with small but shapely branches and very large figs.

Between the hearth and the parasol grew my favorite flowers, scarlet-petaled, black-hearted poppies, and Zeus help the weed which stole their sunlight or the crow which bruised their buds!

I have always felt that a garden should extend and not circumscribe nature; I plant my flowers haphazardly instead of in rows, and sometimes I scatter my tools in pleasant disorder, like branches under a tree. But Thea was used to the tidiness of palace courtyards. I felt rebuked by her look and hurried to pick up a rake, muttering, "I wonder how this got there," though of course I had laid it there myself three weeks ago and stepped around it every morning.

We descended a wooden staircase which coiled below the garden like the winding heart of a conch shell and opened abruptly into my den. One of my Telchines had lit a lamp, which hung from the ceiling by a chain of electrum and swayed in the breeze from the stairs. The walls of the den were roots, twisted and smoothed into shape; and sturdier roots, resembling gnarled pillars, divided the room into separate nooks or dells. You could almost say that I had captured a little corner of the forest. No, not captured. I have never liked that word. Rather, I had trusted myself to the forest, given my safety into the keeping of her labyrinthine roots, which held the earth above my head and below my feet, supported and sustained me. There was beauty in them as well as utility. Just as the convolutions of an old piece of driftwood may leap to color when thrown in a fire, so the brown roots of my house glowed malachite, amber, and lapis lazuli—sea-color, woods-color, sky-color—in the light of a clay lamp. Like Thea's hair, you could say, for brown is not colorless but the reservoir of many colors, which only need to be awakened by the soft fingers of light.

The roots, being dead, were neither moist nor clammy, and the reed mats on the floor, together with a pair of open and gently glowing braziers, lent to the room the warmth and intimacy of a squirrel's nest. Many a night I had tippled beer with my friends until the roots seemed to writhe above us like big friendly snakes, guardian spirits intent on their good offices of cheering and protecting. On other nights, I preferred to read. Of all the room's possessions, my favorite, I think, was the low, cylindrical chest of scrolls—*The Isles of the Blest: Are They Blessed?, Centaur Songs, Hoofbeats in Babylon*—which I read to compensate for my very limited travels (you see, I had never left the forest). As Icarus' great-great uncle might have said, "An untraveled Minotaur is a hungry Minotaur, and reading feedeth him like beer and honey cakes."

But comfortable rooms are rarely neat, and today, hardly expecting guests, I had stacked my cooking utensils, a platter with scraps of bread and a tripod which had held a bird's-nest stew, beside the hand-mill where I ground my grain and occasionally (as today) spilled some flour.

"I will have to see about supper," I said. Remember, I had found no meat in my cave. The carnivorous Telchines would rather turn cannibal than resort to vegetables. "First I will show you your room. I well sleep in here and you may have my bedroom."

It lay at the foot of a ladder: round and snug as a rabbit's burrow; small for me but large for Thea and Icarus. The floor was carpeted with moss and the down of bird's nests. There was no furniture except for a three-legged stool and a citron chest in which I kept a tunic to wear on cold days and a pair of round sandals to shoe my hooves when I went to gather gemstones in the quarry.

Icarus threw himself on the floor and uttered a cry like the neigh of a donkey which has pulled a cart since sunrise and come home at dusk to a bed of straw. "Soft as clover," he said, snuggling into the down and releasing Perdix to find his own nest.

Thea, I saw, did not share his enthusiasm. I had rather expected a compliment on my room, but she thrust an explorative toe into the down to see if it were clean. Suddenly I realized that the room was not designed for a woman.

"We'll find you some toilet articles tomorrow," I promised. "I have a friend with a Babylonian mirror. Shaped like a swan, with the neck for a handle."

"Your room is charming," she said with well-meant insincerity. "You must forgive me if I appear unappreciative. I'm very tired."

"I'll bring you a tub of hot water."

Escaping up the ladder, I remembered the time a fastidious Dryad (not Zoe) had told me that I needed a haircut: all over. Unkempt, I thought, That's what I am, and so is my house.

In the garden, I found the tub which I used for washing vegetables and, thrusting it under the fountain, began to plan my dinner. I could pick some figs and squashes in my garden; I could bake a loaf of bread and gather mushrooms and woodpecker-eggs for an omelette. But what would I do for meat? Perhaps I had time before dark to shoot some hares—

It was then that I heard the scream. When a woman screams, sometimes she means: I need some help but there is no real hurry. It's just my way of attracting attention and pointing up my helplessness. But Thea's scream was sheer, spontaneous terror; it bubbled onto the air like the black poison of hemlock. I jumped down the stairs in three large leaps, slid down the ladder almost without touching the rungs, and found a Telchin crouched at the foot, waving his feelers in consternation. Behind him, Thea was brandishing the three-legged stool and shouting, "Out, out!"

It was of course, her first meeting with a Telchin, a three-foot ant with almost human intelligence and with six skillful legs which make him the best lapidary in the world; he can carve and set gems more delicately than the surest human craftsman. But Thea saw only the great bulbous head, the many-faceted eyes, the black, armored skin.

"It crawled down the ladder," she said in a whisper. "Then it came at me, waving its feelers."

"He didn't come at you, he came looking for me," I snapped emphasizing the *he*, for I saw that her scornful *it* had hurt his feelings. "And he understands every word you say. He is quite harmless except to other Telchines." I stroked his antennae. He indicated pacification with a pleased buzzing which vibrated through my fingers. Icarus, belatedly rousing himself from his nap, climbed to his feet and walked without hesitation to the trembling Telchin. He knelt and leaned his head against the creature's armor.

"What's his name?" he asked.

"Telchines hide their names except from their mates. I call him Bion."

"Bion," said Icarus. "I want you to meet Perdix." The teased buzzing became a roar.

Thea, meanwhile, had started to cry.

"Don't cry," I said. "He's forgiven you now."

"But I'm still afraid. Of—of everything in the forest!"

"Of me?"

She looked at me for a long moment before she spoke. "At first, in the cave. Even after Icarus said you were friendly. Not any more, though. Not since I saw our flowers. But the forest terrifies me. I thought I was safe down here, and then I saw Bion, and it seemed as if the forest had followed me."

"It had," I said, "but the good part. The forest is like a Man or a Beast, with many moods. Bion would rather hurt his brother than hurt my guests. Wouldn't you, Bion?"

"I'm a terrible coward, Eunostos."

"You were very brave when you met me in the cave. You waved your fist in my face."

"I seemed to be brave, but I wasn't really. My heart was jumping like a startled quail."

"It doesn't matter what your heart does so long as your feet stand still. In the last two days your heart has had good reason to jump. You have lost your home, crashed in a glider, fallen into the clutches of Ajax, and faced the Minotaur in his cave. But all those things are behind you."

"Yes." She smiled. "You will protect me here. I see that now."

She was the first real lady to look on me for protection. I did not know, however, that she planned to improve my manners and redecorate my house.

Chapter IV

DOMESTICATIONS AND DOMESTICITY

She never said to me, "Eunostos, you ought to comb your hair or get a new pair of sandals." It was always "Perhaps you should…" or "Don't you think…" Sometimes she worked through her brother. Two weeks after their arrival he told me in confidence, "Thea hasn't complained, but I think she misses Cretan plumbing."

"But she has a hot shower," I protested. "Or else I bring her a tub. What more does she want?"

"What she wants is a bathroom," he confided. It is universally acknowledged that the Cretans are the best plumbers in all the lands of the great Green Sea. Not only do they pipe water into their palaces, but they build limestone toilets with wooden seats and, wonder of wonders, a lever for flushing. Like my ancestors, I am something of an engineer, and I lost no time in diverting a part of the spring from the garden. With her usual delicacy, Thea did not refer to my innovation, but she showed her gratitude by making me a pair of leather sandals which pinched my hooves like chains on a mule. At least in the house, I had to wear them or hurt her feelings.

Once out of the house, however, I kicked them under a tree and happily pursued my business in the forest; now that my cave no longer received a weekly sacrifice—the local farmers, it seemed, were feeding the conquerors instead of the Minotaur—I hunted daily to keep my guests in meat. But one such hunt landed me in a much more serious predicament than the mere discomfort of sandals. I had bagged a wild pig with my first arrow and started back to the house with the carcass strapped across my shoulder.

"Ho there," a voice boomed from the trees, and Moschus, the Centaur, cantered up beside me with thumping hooves and a swirl of dust. A robust fellow, Moschus, in spite of his years. His flanks glistened with olive oil; powerful muscles rippled beneath his coat; chestnut hair tumbled down the back of his neck in a glossy mane. It was true that his hair had begun to thin, for Moschus was a good two hundred years old; he had been a colt in the days when the Beasts had lived on the coast, sharing their secrets with the fast-learning and still friendly Cretans. But age became him as it did the oaks and the cedars.

Physically, at least. His intelligence, never high, had begun to decline before I was born. His noble exterior suggested learning and promised wise utterances, but his only interests were wenching, storytelling (bawdy), and playing the flute, and his conversation was threadbare on all other subjects.

"Heard about you and the kids," he said.

"Oh," I said, noncommittal. "Did you?" I did not want him to suggest a meeting. Thea would not understand his libertine ways.

"Big daddy himself. Though I hear the girl is not exactly a child (heh)."

"Not in years," I said loftily. "but she's led a sheltered life."

"Time for a party then—lower the parasol! How about to-night?"

"Busy. Tanning hides." I pointed to the pig on my shoulder.

"Tomorrow night?"

"Cutting gems."

A look of suspicion narrowed his equine eyes. "I thought your workers did that."

"Too many gems; not enough help."

"The next night?"

"At your house?" I sighed, defeated.

"You're a better host. More beer, more room. Zoe and I will come after lamplighting time."

"Zoe too?"

"Who else? You know we're keeping company." With a loud, anticipatory neigh, he galloped into the trees.

I groaned. Zoe, the Dryad, and Moschus, the Centaur. I loved them devotedly as friends, but together they well might precipitate an orgy.

I knelt to retrieve my sandals, wondering how I could broach the party to Thea.

I found her visiting with my three workers. With the help of Icarus and several bribes of raw meat, she had won their confidence—at least, their acceptance—and often watched them work. Not only were they lapidaries, but blacksmiths, weavers, dyers, shoemakers, and tanners, and their various tools of trade—loom, forge, anvil, assorted vats and tables—lent to my shop the air of a small but handily equipped marketplace. To see only three of them with so much equipment had astonished Thea until I explained that I myself was the fourth worker and, like my extinct countrymen, equal to any four Men or two Telchines. It was not a boast but a simple statement of fact.

The shop was illuminated by six large lamps in the shape of fishtailed ships which navigated the air on swaying chains. One of the workers stood at the forge, holding a bent dagger over the flames; another worked at a table, cleaning the dirt and shale from gemstones; and the third examined a large carnelian, smoothed to the round flatness of a seal, and bobbed his head in evident perplexity.

Thea was watching the holder of the stone as he turned it over and over between his multiple legs. The room was warm with the heat of the forge, but she looked immaculate in her saffron kilt; as far as I knew she never perspired. Three meticulously arranged curls adorned her forehead like pendant snails.

"Eunostos," she said. "Have you ever seen such a gem?" Its smoky gray surface imprisoned the six fires of the lamps in a small constellation, and the many-faceted eyes of the Telchin reflected them again to numbers beyond counting.

"Would you like it to wear as a ring?" I asked.

She looked like a child who has just been offered a dolphin or a rare, white-plumed griffin. "Oh, yes, but don't you trade these things to the other Beasts?" I had told her how every Beast contributed to the self-sufficiency of the forest: I traded my gems to the Centaurs for seeds to plant in my garden; the Dryads built wooden chests and swapped them to the Thriae for the honey stored in their great hexagons; and even the little Bears of Artemis gathered black-eyed Susans in the fields and strung necklaces to trade for dolls.

"Not this one," I said. "What design would you like?"

She thought. "A blue monkey," Her eyes looked beyond me, wistful no doubt with memories of the palace at Vathypetro, the well-ordered garden, and of course her father. "Is that possible?"

"A blue monkey and—" I whispered to the Telchin. In spite of their skill, they are not inventive, and unless you give them suggestions, they will settle on one design and duplicate it a hundred or more times. Nodding sagely, he set to work with a pointed file.

"May I watch?" Thea asked.

"No," I said. "Surprises are best." And then, unobtrusively: "Thea, some friends are coming to call. After supper, two nights from now."

She reserved judgment. "How many?"

"Just two. A Centaur and a Dryad."

"Zoe," she said. "You've mentioned her several times." It was almost an accusation.

"An old friend," I explained.

"Older than you?"

"Let's see. About fourteen times as old."

"Elderly then."

"Not exactly. Dryads reflect the state of their trees. Zoe's oak is well-preserved."

She stifled a sigh. "But have we enough wine in the house?"

"Beer," I said. "Beer is what they drink. Both of them."

"A woman drinks beer?"

"She can outdrink me!" Then subdued: "I brew it from barley right here in the ship. You ought to try some."

She smiled magnanimously. "Perhaps I will. You attend to the beer and I will bake some honey cakes." She paused. "It's good I've finished your new tunic."

"Tunic?" I cried. In the spring and summer, no male Beast wore clothes. Why should he? The air which blew from the torrid continent of Libya was warm and dry, and female Beasts were no more disturbed by a free expanse of masculine flesh than Cretan males by the bare breasts of their women.

"Yes," she said, fishing the depths of a basket with nimble fingers. "The Telchines wove it, but I did the dyeing and needlework."

"I see you did." Lavender, with embroidered sleeves. "Why not a loincloth?"

"For Icarus, perhaps, not for you. You are—well, more mature." She observed the hair on my chest as if she were thinking of scissors. "Try it on now and see if it fits."

The tunic pinched me in seven places. I felt like a snake imprisoned in his old, discarded skin. "I can't move." I said. "I can't breath. I think I'm going to suffocate. And," I added delicately, "you forgot to leave access for my tail."

"Hush. All it needs is a bit of taking out." She proceeded to pinch and pat me as if I were no more animate than a side of beef. "Or else you could reduce, if only the party were next week instead of in two nights."

"I can't postpone it," I snapped. "Besides, I'm not fat, I'm muscular." I guided her hand to the stomach as firm and hard as a coconut.

"You're right. Sheer muscle. I'll have to let out the waist."

As soon as I entered the den, I saw a change. Ever since Thea's arrival, the room had been orderly: No more unwashed dishes stacked by the grainmill; for that matter, no more mill, which now scattered its flour beside the fountain. The change at the moment, however, had been added rather than subtracted. In the glow of a freshly lit lamp, three dove-shaped vases nested among the roots and bristled with poppies out of my garden. The sad little heads of my flowers stared reproachfully from every corner of the room, five heads to a dove.

"You've killed them," I cried. "You've cut their throats."

"Housed, not killed. In the garden, nobody noticed them."

"I did. Every day. Here it's like putting them in jail."

"I shall try to be a kind jailer," she smiled, straightening a flower.

At the mention of jailer, I recalled my own imprisonment in the tunic. Her alterations had not improved the fit, nor had she remembered the access of my tail, which pressed stiffly against my back like a sun-dried reed. As soon as she turned her back to straighten another flower, I filled my chest with air, hoping to burst my belt and split the tunic. I only increased my discomfort. I stared with envy at Icarus in his new loin-cloth, which was green and unembroidered. He looked both spruce and comfortable. Thea herself wore a blue, divided skirt almost to her ankles, each side falling in tiers embossed with gold-leaf. Her hair, combed as always to hide her ears, rippled in three rivulets down her back like cascading autumn leaves with faint twinkles of summer's departed green. On her middle finger she wore the agate ring which the Telchin had already finished incising, not only with a blue monkey but with a Cretan maiden who was unmistakably Thea, receiving from her pet the gift of a crocus. From my whispered description of her garden at Vathypetro, the artist had realized the scene beyond my expectations. After cutting the figures, he had filled them with microscopic particles of lapis lazuli. A scene of play, you would think, but the austere blue stone imparted a dignity and sadness which seemed to say: playful moments endure only in stone.

"It's exquisite," she said, caressing the ring as if it were an amulet to ensure fertility. She came to me and, standing on tiptoe, grasped my horn and drew my cheek to her lips.

"Dear Eunostos, you are like a brother to me. I'm glad I had the tunic to give you in return. Otherwise, I could never have accepted such an expensive gift."

Above our heads the cowbell tinkled the arrival of our guests.

"We must let them in," said Thea.

I shook my head. "I had better meet them alone. Moschus needs plenty of room on the stairs." I did not want her to hear their comments about my tunic.

But one of my workers, roasting a late chip in the garden, had already opened the door, and Zoe thumped down the stairs like a sack of coconuts. Moschus labored behind her, managing his four legs with obvious difficulty, and I half expected to see him lose his balance and tumble head over hooves. At the end of her descent, Zoe caught me in a huge embrace. I submitted rather than responded. Not that I scorned a friendly hug. More than once we had frolicked away the night in the windy heights of her tree. But Thea was watching us with cool, unblinking eyes.

"Thea," I said, "I want you to meet my friends, Zoe and Moschus."

"Little Thea," cried Zoe, opening her arms for another engulfment, and I feared for Thea's ribs.

Smiling thinly, Thea offered her hand. "Eunostos has told me about you."

Zoe looked at her as if with recognition. "Your ears," she said, "Are they—?"

Thea evaded the question. "And Moschus," she said, as she reached to steady him down the last stair. "How good of you to come."

"Isn't he pretty," cried Zoe, discovering Icarus in time to hide her embarrassment over Thea's rebuff. "Eunostos, you should have sent me word. I would have worn sandals." She was barefoot as usual and dressed in a gown as dingy and mottled as an old wineskin. When she held out her hand to Icarus, her shell bracelets jangled like tin gewgaws from the

Misty Isles. Icarus ignored the hand and gave her the kind of hug she had given me. A radiant smile suffused her face and flaunted the three gold teeth which a Babylonian dentist, her three-hundredth lover, had left her when they parted. She patted the boy on the head.

"Head's not as big as I thought." She laughed when his mass of hair depressed beneath her fingers. "But there's plenty of room for brains." She looked at me and winked. "Though there might be things I could teach him, eh, Eunostos?"

Icarus was fascinated. The generosity of her breasts, like an overhanging cliff, magnetized his gaze; he seemed to expect a landslide. "I'm a good pupil." He grinned.

Then she turned to me. "Eunostos, have you gotten fat?"

"Certainly not," I said. In truth, I had lost six pounds since Thea's arrival.

"Then why do you hide your belly in that—tunic, is it called?"

"Lavender," snickered Moschus, "Embroidered (heh!)."

"It's a present," said Thea. "From me."

"One of the city styles, I expect," said Zoe. "Well, it's good to keep abreast of the fashions. But, Eunostos, I miss that manly chest."

But Zoe and Moschus were not our only guests. A minikin figure, no more obtrusive than a shadow, crouched at the foot of the stairs. I recognized Pandia, one of the Bears of Artemis.

"She met us in the woods and wanted to come," apologized Zoe. "Since she doesn't drink, you'll hardly know she's here."

She was four feet tall. Her hair was short; in fact, it was fur, but neatly trimmed so that it resembled a felt cap. She wore a fillet of sweetbriar, a necklace of green acorns, a tunic of woodpecker feathers caught at the waist by a belt of rabbit skin, and a pair of kidskin sandals from my own workshop. Her nub of a tail protruded from a small hole in the back of her tunic. Before the coming of Men, it was said, the goddess Artemis had visited Crete and given her love to a bear. Just as the offspring of Pan are the little hooved Panisci, so the off-spring of Artemis are the stub-tailed bears, and the two tribes, who keep their childlike bodies throughout their long lives, mix and propagate from the age of fourteen. Pandia, though, was no more than the ten years she looked.

"Do you mind?" she asked in a small but husky voice. "I heard about the party from one of your workers and came to watch. I don't drink, you know."

"She came to keep me company," said Icarus, though he himself had every intention of drinking. "We've already met from a distance. The day Thea and I crashed in the glider." You might have thought that a boy of fifteen would disdain the company of a little girl, but Icarus never seemed to notice the difference in people's ages. He had a remarkable gift for making youth feel mature and old age young. Foregoing Zoe and her monumental cliffs, he drew Pandia to a bench with moss-filled cushions.

"Here we can watch without getting stepped on," he said.

"When I saw you crash," she was saying, "I expected to find just bodies and have to beat off the crows! Then the soldiers came and dragged you off to their camp."

Among my other guests, conversation had died; rather, it had not survived the first stiff exchange of formalities. Zoe's exuberance had faded to a wan smile, and Moschus, who had misinterpreted Thea's help on the stairs, had fixed the girl in a silent, lecherous stare.

"Time for a drink," I called like any practiced host, and pointed to a large, pitch-covered goatskin of beer, with an up-raised hoof for a spout. I handed Zoe a cup and lifted the skin.

"You know I don't need a cup," she said, and took the skin from my hands. Tilting her head, she placed the foot to her mouth and threatened to empty the contents with one re-sounding gurgle. A thin trickle of beer meandered down her neck and vanished between her breasts like a freshet between two mountains.

"Here, let Moschus have a drink," I said at last. "He looks parched."

Interspersing his gulps with appreciative "heh's," Moschus drank his fill and relinquished the skin. "Thea?" I asked.

"Why not?" Carefully she wiped off the foot with a linen handkerchief and poured a modest portion into a cup. Dainty as a bird drinking dew from a leaf, she quaffed the liquid.

"Tastes like good old vintage," she said, resisting a wry face.

"Vintage?" Moschus grinned. "That's beer, dear, and it's fresh from the vat."

To cover Thea's embarrassment, I seized the skin and raised the hoof to my lips. "Moschus, start the music," I cried between gulps. He withdrew a flute from his sole item of clothing, a wolfskin sash, and began to play. The flute was a crude cylinder of tortoise shell, but Moschus' music was wild, sweet, and eloquent with many voices: the slow creaking groan of palm trees in the wind; the tumble of waves subsiding into a long-drawn hiss; the hoot of an owl; the shriek of a hunting wolf. Zoe motioned an invitation to Icarus.

"Go ahead," said Pandia. "I don't dance."

He occupied Zoe's arms, and she led the boy in a sinuous undulation which alternated with leaps in the air and throaty cries of "Evoe, Evoe!"

"The Dance of the Python!" he cried with recognition. "But we haven't a snake." He darted from the floor and Zoe, muttering about the vagaries of youth, cast about for a new partner. I was ready to offer myself when Icarus returned with Perdix. "Our Python!"

"Pipe that flute!" cried Zoe, and she flung back her head till her green, gray-streaked tresses bobbed like the snakes of a Gorgon. She was three hundred and sixty-nine years old (a lover for each year, she claimed), and like her tree she looked as if many a woodpecker had mottled her skin and many a storm weatherbeaten her complexion; but beauty had not forsaken her: the full-blown beauty of an earth mother whose ample lap could pillow a lover's head and whose opulent breasts could suckle a score of children. She stirred my blood like a skin of beer.

"My turn," I called.

Restraining fingers caught at my belt. "Mine," said Thea.

"I'll step on your toes," I protested, edging toward Zoe.

"Not in my dance." Her fingers were irresistible. "We call it the Walk of the Cranes." We linked hands and she led me through stately, meandering steps like those of the young virgins when they dance beside the River Kairatos, though the music seemed more appropriate to the opium-drugged priestesses of the Great Mother, when they yield themselves to ecstasy, writhe on the ground, and tear the bark from a tree with their savage teeth.

"Your friends are very"—she paused to select a word—"exuberant. I'm afraid they will tire my brother."

"He seems to be holding his own," I observed as the boy and his partner, her capacious bulk grown seemingly weightless, mimicked snakes on the ground and birds in the air, leaped with exultant cries of "Evoe! Evoe!"

"Eunostos," she said. "Do you like my dance?"

"Well, it has dignity."

"Yes, but sometimes you men seem to like something more animalistic." A wistfulness softened her voice. She looked even less than her sixteen years, a very young girl whose knowledge of men was limited to a father, a brother, and a few palace retainers. I tightened my grip on her hand.

"I think," she said sadly, "that most men like innocence only because it challenges them to change it into experience."

"Physical innocence, yes," I said. "That we like to change—after all it is merely ignorance. But the innocence of the heart—that is as rare as the black pearls from the land of the Yellow Men, and no honorable Beast wishes to threaten it, any more than he would drop a pearl in a glass of wine and watch it dissolve."

"But the body encloses the heart. When the body falls, what dignity is left to the heart?"

"None, when the body falls; but when it is given, like a proud city to a noble king, then it grows rich—then it enriches the heart."

Against the feverish background of the flute, our shouted words seemed strangely impersonal, strangely divorced from the girl and Beast who spoke them. When the music ended, our words faltered in the great silence.

"That's all," said Moschus, wiping his lips and returning the flute to his wolfskin sash. "Musician wants a drink." But he came at Thea with a thirst which was not for beer.

She disengaged her hand and hurried up the stairs toward the garden and the oven.

Moschus glared after her. "Skittish colt, eh, Eunostos?"

She returned with a heaping aviary of cakes in the form of owls, woodpeckers, swallows, eagles, and partridges, whose piquant scents enwreathed the platter and titillated our nostrils. She was justly proud of her baking.

"Not for me, honey," said Zoe, heading for the beer. "I don't eat while I'm drinking. Spoils the kick."

"Same here," said Moschus, slapping Zoe's flank.

Thea's smile vanished. Her one contribution to the party was being ignored. "Pandia?" she asked doubtfully. Pandia sprang to her feet and converged on the birds, scooping them into her mouth so quickly that they seemed to flutter from the plate.

"You see why I don't drink," she said as she licked the last crumbs from her stubby hands (paws, should I say?). "It would waterlog the food."

Now the drinking began in earnest. Six times I had to replenish the skin, while Thea followed me, mopping the beer which trickled onto the floor. Moschus watched her and brooded over what he whispered was youth's lack of appreciation for mature years. "She treats me like an old dray," he muttered. Icarus rested his head in Zoe's lap; with one hand, she trickled beer down his throat from a rhyton shaped like a bull, with the other she stroked his pointed ears.

"Sly little Beast," she said in a hoarse whisper. "Why did you take so long to come back to the forest?"

Between swallows he raised his head and caught Pandia's eye. "All right, Pandy?" he called.

Pandia nodded vehemently. She had the look of a child who has caught her parents drinking, but there was no disapproval in the wide, watchful eyes; there was expectation of further excesses.

An increasingly nervous host, I alternated between swigs of beer and anxious looks at Thea, whose expression was dire enough to dismay a Gorgon. Suddenly I felt defiant. It was my house and my friends, and she had no right to mistake our good-natured mischief for misbehaving. A little horse-play on the part of Moschus; Zoe expansively maternal but hardly wanton; Icarus enjoying himself and Pandia enjoying the view. What was the harm in that? I sat down on the rug beside Zoe and twined an arm around the hill of her shoulders. Without displacing Icarus, she lent me the arm with which she had stroked his ears.

"Moschus, there's room for you too," she called with perhaps excessive optimism.

"Thea," I bellowed. "Fetch us some more beer! Your guests are thirsty."

A cold streamer of beer swatted me across the mouth.

"You're drunk," snapped Thea, "and so is Icarus," and, turning to Zoe: "You're to blame!"

Zoe's voice was relaxed. "Dear, your brother is fifteen and it's time he learned to hold his liquor. As for Eunostos, he's hardly begun to drink. You ought to see him after another skin!" She gave a body-wrenching sigh. "However, I expect it's time to go. It's a long way to my tree, and there are Striges about at night, to say nothing of those thieving Thriae." Still unhurried, with the slow deliberate movements of a mother placing her baby in a crib, she lifted Icarus' head from her lap and cradled it on a cushion.

He looked up at her with sleepy disappointment. "Your lap was softer."

She winked. "Boy, when you want a lap instead of a cushion, come to my tree. It's a royal oak. Eunostos knows the way!"

I saw them up the stairs and across the garden. The silver palm of the fountain swayed in the moonlight; the crude parasol stood like the silk pavilion of an Eastern king; and even the homely oven looked dim and mysterious, fit for incense instead of bread. But the headless stalks of my poppies made me sad, in spite of the moon and its white, ennobling foam.

"Zoe," I said. "Moschus. You will have to forgive her. She isn't used to our ways."

"You think that's it?" Zoe smiled. "Inexperience, innocence, and all that? I would have said she was jealous."

"Of Icarus?"

"Of you."

Chapter V

KORA

I awoke to singing. The singer was Thea in the garden, and her song was about a tiger moth:

His heart is dappled like his wing:
Day-yellow spilled with night.
The tiger-part loves evening,
The moth-part, candlelight.

I disentangled myself from a pile of wolfskins, yawned mightily, and climbed the stairs to investigate her high spirits.

In the garden she was pulling my last carrots out of their earthen burrows. I winced. Of course they were grown to be eaten, but after the decapitation of my poppies, I resented any diminishment of my shrunken plot. Blue monkeys had lined the walls to watch her, and one bold fellow had skittered onto the ground to receive a carrot. I glared at his boldness but only managed to increase his appetite.

She climbed to her feet and smiled. "We're going on a picnic. I'm getting lunch ready now."

"What should I wear?" I asked. I had not taken time to dress.

"You are dressed exactly right," she said. "Picnics should be informal."

With a lunch of hard-boiled woodpecker eggs, roasted chestnuts, wolf's milk cheese, raw carrots (the last of their race), and honey cakes, together with a flask of wine encased in wickerwork, we headed for the Field of the Gem Stones. Icarus was still drowsy when we left the house, I had carried him up the stairs and held him under the fountain, but the warm water had barely roused him enough to move his feet in a kind of lethargic shuffle. Thea and I talked freely, however, and as soon as our conversation turned to those incorrigible thieves, the Thriae, he began to listen.

"Their women are very beautiful," I said, "If you don't mind golden eyes and billowy wings. But never fall in love with one."

"Why not?" he asked.

"Because," I began, but then we came to the Field of Gem Stones, and I left his question unanswered. Imagine a field which Tital horses have ploughed, with furrows like the troughs of waves in a tempest and enormous boulders poised like ships on the crests. Actually an earthquake had ravaged the land instead of giants, and vegetation—grass, thickets of sweetbriar, and poppies with scarlet heads—had soothed without quite healing the wounded soil; had clung to the curves, the abrupt rises, the sharp pinnacles with wild green tenacity. Thea admired the poppies—picked one, in fact—but shuddered at the savagery of the landscape.

"The earth looks angry," she said. "It is not the handiwork of the Great Mother, but one of those northern gods, Pluto perhaps. It might be his very playground."

"But it's private," I said. "And safe. The furrows shut us from view. The Panisci, you know, love to heckle picnickers. One of them attracts your attention with his goatish antics and his friends make off with the lunch." I brushed off a stone for her seat. "Chalcedony. I'll take it home with us, and my workers will cut you a necklace. You can find just about any-thing you want here—carnelian, agate, jasper."

No sooner had I laid our basket on a tuft of grass than a small felt hat bobbed above the nearest ridge. No, it was Pandia's hair.

"I smelled cakes," she said. "They smell like more than you can eat."

"Come and join us," said Icarus, nobly if reluctantly, since the cakes in fact were less than we could eat. Thea had yet to learn the extent of a Minotaur's appetite.

"Too many are bad for you," Pandia explained. "One of my acquaintances—not a friend, fortunately—gorged herself and got so sweet that a hungry bear came out of the trees and ate her. Ate his own cousin. Didn't leave a crumb." As always before a meal, she looked immaculate. She had spruced her tail, cleaned her kidskin sandals, and tied her belt of rabbit's fur in a neat bow with exactly equal ends.

"I've thought of a poem about bears," I said. "It goes:

Bears like berries
Ras- and blue-,
Speckled trout,
And catfish too.
Best of all,
Bears like snacks
Smuggled out of
Picnic packs!

And here's one about that dreadful bear that ate your acquaintance.

Brownest, broadest,
Hungriest, hairiest—
Of all the bears,
He is beariest."

"I like your poems, Eunostos," said Pandia. "They are almost as charming as your tail, which is very slender and elegant. But all that business about eating has made me too hungry to appreciate any more recitation."

Icarus handed her our entire supply of honey cakes, packaged in a linen handkerchief. "There are no bears in the neighborhood," he said.

She ate most of the cakes between two breaths and stuffed the remnants into her tunic.

"Shall we gather stones?" asked Icarus. "The Telchines will polish them for us. We can use our picnic basket."

"I would like an amulet to ward off the Striges," she admitted, and followed him up the ridge, fishing a fragment of cake out of her tunic.

Thea, meanwhile, nibbled a carrot so fastidiously that she managed to avoid a crunch. A persistent wind frolicked the hair from her ears and the hand which was not occupied with the carrot replaced the hair.

"Thea," I said, "you look like a circumspect rabbit."

She smiled and wriggled her nose. "But I don't have whiskers."

Then she was not a rabbit but utterly a woman, so soft of hair, so tiny of hand, that I wanted to cry and be comforted on her bosom like a sad child.

"Thea," I whispered.

"Yes, Eunostos."

"Thea, I—"

"Would you like a carrot?"

"No."

"How do you grow them so crisp and yellow?"

"Fertilizer," I said. "Fish heads, mostly." At that point a god or demon possessed me, like the quick flush of heat from the sun which breaks through the clouds on a chilly day. I removed the carrot from Thea's fingers and then I embraced her. To me, the action seemed as natural as taking a shower in the hot plume of my fountain or kneeling in my garden to measure the bud of a poppy. But possessed as I was by the god (or demon), I forgot my strength. Perhaps I was rough; certainly I was sudden. She lay in my arms like a fawn pierced by an arrow. I have broken her back, I thought. Crushed her fragility with my brutish lust, as if I had taken a swallow's egg in my palm and closed my fingers.

"Thea," I groaned, loosening my grip but still supporting her body. "Are you—"

With unhurried dignity, she disengaged herself from my arms. "Eunostos, I am ashamed of you. You are acting like Moschus."

Better to be insulted, railed against, slapped, than chastised like a naughty child or a mischievous Centaur. Moschus indeed!

Angrily I blurted: "He kisses everyone he meets at the first chance. You've shared my house for a month, and I haven't touched you until today. But I'm not a eunuch."

"I look on you as a brother. I told you that."

"But I don't want to be your brother. I don't feel fraternal at all. Besides, you already have Icarus. I want to be—"

"My father? It's true you're ten years older—"

"No, that's worse. I don't like your father anyway."

"You don't like him? But you never met him. He's a kingly man!"

"I do know him," I said. "I wasn't going to tell you, but I knew him before you were born."

She gasped. "In the forest?"

"And I knew your mother, the Dryad."

"I don't think I want to hear about her."

"I can't tell you about your father without mentioning your mother." I called loudly: "Icarus, Pandia!"

They hurried over the ridge with dirty hands and a basket of stones between them.

"Is it bears?" whispered Pandia with terror-rounded eyes. "Are we going to be eaten?"

"Not bears," I said. "Something I want to show you."

A mile from the Field of Stones, in a small clearing green with moss and fern I showed them a fire-blackened stump which had once been a royal oak.

Through the gutted walls, you could see the ruined beginnings of a staircase, spiraling around the trunk and ending abruptly in air.

"Your mother's tree." I said. And I told them about Aeacus, their father.

* * * *

I was nine years old when he came to the forest. My father had built a house of reeds in a tamarisk grove, and after my mother was killed by lightning, we lived alone with the feathery trees shutting away the sunlight and shutting us in the shadows of our loss. Except at night when I needed a place to sleep, I kept away from the house, preferring to roam the woods where I had gathered chestnuts with my mother and listened to her stories about the coming of our people from the Isles of the Blest. It was in the forest that I met Aeacus—dagger in hand, blood on his beardless face, eyes vacant like those of a Strige's victim. I learned later that he had come into the mountains pursuing Achaean pirates. He and his men met and killed them just beyond the forest, but only Aeacus had survived the skirmish. Wounded and delirious, he had wandered into the forest, but strength had failed him and he sank to his knees like a murderer before a judge, dripping his dagger, blinking without awareness.

I crept out of the undergrowth. "May I help you, sir?" I asked from a safe distance, for he was a Man and therefore dangerous.

"He cannot speak." A tall Dryad had come to stand beside me.

"Your dress is sunlight!" I cried.

"Sunflowers," She smiled. "Every morning I weave it anew, since the petals endure only for a day. Like love."

"And your hair is a green waterfall. It sings around your shoulders."

"Perhaps," she said, "it has learned its song from the trees in which I live. Listened to woodpeckers nesting in the branches, or those smaller birds, the wind-ruffled leaves. But now we must help our friend."

"He's a Man," I whispered. She did not look as if she understood the danger.

"And therefore the more to be pitied."

His hair, worn long and drawn behind his head in a fillet, was a wonder of darkness, and his face was as white and smooth as the alabaster from which the Cretans carve the thrones of their kings: such a face as the artisan god, Hephaestus, might carve in his underground workshop—unflawed by toil, untouched by time.

Each of us took an arm and supported him to her tree. She did not invite me to enter the trunk. She smiled when she saw my disappointment; for I had heard of the marvels within a Dryad's tree: the winding stairs cut into the trunk, the secret doors which opened onto rooms where noiseless spiders weave in the light of glowworms, the platforms among the branches, where the Dryads comb their tresses to the soft fingerings of the sun.

"You must not enter, Bull Boy. I am bringing sorrow into my tree, and you have enough of your own."

"He will do you injury?"

"Perhaps."

"Why do you shelter him then?"

"I have lived too long in sunlight."

No Man can enter the forest without alerting the Beasts. All of us, even the light-fingered Thriae and the careless Panisci, take our turns patrolling the narrow access to the world of Men. Everywhere else the cliffs uprear impassable walls (except for my cave, which no one dares to invade). When Aeacus entered the trees, I was not the first to see him. Even as Kora helped him into her house, a conch-shell boomed a warning to all the Beasts, and the next day Chiron, king of the Centaurs, arrived at her tree to question her about the stranger.

"I am going to bear his child," she said.

Chiron was stunned. A human father and a bestial mother! Would the child be a Man or a Beast? Shaking his mane, he left this foolish Dryad to the sorrow of her own choosing.

I was ten years old at the birth of Thea, eleven when Icarus followed her into the tree and laughed with his first breath. High in the branches, a porch surrounded the trunk, with a bench and bamboo rail. I used to stand on the ground and wait until Kora appeared with the babies.

"Eunostos," she called one morning. "Come and visit with me."

"Through the door?" I asked, hoping at least to glimpse the interior.

"Up the outside ladder."

I saw with dismay that her hair looked as withered as broken ferns, and her gown was woven of brown leaves instead of sunflower petals. She lifted Thea into my arms.

"Is she breakable?" I asked doubtfully.

"Not unless you drop her out of the tree." She laughed.

At first Thea was crying. "I expect it's my hair," I said. "The color has frightened her."

"No," she said. "It's the forest. She always cries when I bring her onto the porch."

I took her tiny hand and placed the fingers on one of my horns. "See," I said. "It won't hurt you. It is like a carrot."

She fell asleep in my arms.

"I want to hold Icarus too," I said. "One baby for each arm. They will balance each other." He was much the fattest baby I had ever seen. When no one held him, he would lie in the crib which his mother had hollowed from the shell of a tortoise and coo at friendly woodpeckers or empty air. He made me think of a fledgling which has gorged itself on worms and grown so plump that it has no wish to fly. It would rather stay in the nest and wait for the next worm.

Without telling their mother, I adored both of them—Thea because she was sad, Icarus because he was plump and joyful. Sometimes Kora would let me look after them when she followed Aeacus into the forest (it must have broken her heart to see him walk to the edge of the trees and stare wistfully at the farms across the meadow). I fed them nectar which I squeezed out of honeysuckle blossoms and made up stories in which I rescued them from wicked bears and slavering wolves. They seemed attentive, both of them, and never fell asleep until I had finished my story, though few of my words could have been intelligible to such young ears.

Soon after Icarus' first birthday, I climbed to the porch and discovered Kora in tears. Since the death of my mother, I had seen my father cry and I knew that the tears of adults were wetter, saltier, and much, much sadder than those of a child like me. I started down the ladder.

"Stay, Eunostos," she said. "It will be your last chance to see the children."

I balanced awkwardly on the third rung from the top and rested my chin on the porch. "I'm not to be invited again?"

"They are going away."

"How can you go with them?" I knew that no Dryad could leave her tree for more than a few days. Its wooden walls sustain her as salt water sustains a dolphin.

"Their father is taking them to Knossos without me."

"To the cities of Men!" I cried with dismay. Remember that Beast children fear Men as much as human children fear Beasts. I imagined the babies spitted on sharp spears and served up at a banquet, or lowered on giant fish hooks to bait sharks.

"Their father will protect them," she said. "But they will miss us, won't they, my little Bull?"

"Can they live outside the tree?"

"Aeacus thinks so. He says they have not grown dependent on the tree as I have. That's why he wishes to take them now, before they do." She drew me into her arms as if I were one of her own children.

"Don't be sad," I said, though her news was the worst I had heard since the death of my mother. I rested my horns against the leaf-sweet fragrance of her breast.

Neither of us heard Aeacus climb the ladder. He was not angry; he had no reason for anger. But he looked like a staring pharaoh carved from stone. He drew me from Kora's arms and placed me on the ladder. His fingers were very hard, almost like coral, though he did not hurt me. As I started down the ladder, I screamed:

"You shouldn't take them away from their mother!"

For six mornings I went to Kora's tree, placed an ear to the trunk, and listened to Thea's cries resounding through the bark. But no one appeared on the porch to ask me up the ladder, and when I knocked at the door on the seventh morning, Aeacus answered and closed the door in my face.

The next day I met him in the forest. You have seen the twin panniers on the backs of donkeys? They are baskets for carrying produce home from the market or kindling from the woods. He had rigged such panniers for his children and placed both Thea and Icarus on his back. In spite of the vines which strangled the branches above her head, Thea was poised and smiling, but Icarus was crying almost for the first time.

I sprang out of the trees like the goat-god Pan when he frightens travelers. "Where are you taking my babies?" I demanded in what I meant to be an earsplitting bellow. But I was small at the time—I lived on roots and berries between the rare occasions when my father remembered to hunt. No doubt my roar emerged as a squeak. Aeacus looked at me vaguely and went on his way as if I were no more significant than a toadstool. I lowered my head and butted him with my horns, expecting to catch the babies if they threatened to spill. He staggered but kept his balance and did not spill them. Turning, he seized my horns and flung me into the bushes. The fall left me stunned.

In seconds, or minutes, I am not sure which, I opened my eyes to hairy haunches and cloven hooves. A Paniscus, looking about twelve but possibly as old as a hundred, was dousing my face with milk from a split coconut. I did not remember to thank him, but sprang to my feet and searched frantically for signs of Aeacus and the children.

"Did you see him?" I cried. "The man from the Cities?"

"Nothing but squirrels." He sulked, hurt no doubt because I had not thanked him for reviving me and sacrificing the milk from his coconut.

I ran toward Kora's tree to see if she knew that Aeacus had taken the children. Perhaps, I thought, she will keep me in their place, and then I felt terribly ashamed at having so selfish a wish at such a time.

A score of Beasts had surrounded the tree: Dryads in great dishevelment, among them Zoe; Moschus and two other Centaurs; Panisci and Bears of Artemis; and even some Thriae, who flock to misfortune as readily as to honey. The tree was a pillar of fire. Branches crackled and fell in a swarm of sparks like glowing bees; the watchers shielded their heads with upraised arms and drew back from the yellow, lashing coils. The high porch had shriveled like a dead insect and begun to peel from the trunk. Yet the verdurous branches still struggled valiantly to hold their greenness against the encroaching fire, for the tree was young by the reckoning of the forest and three times her lightning-blackened branches had sprouted leaves.

"We must save her," I cried, running toward the ladder.

Zoe stopped me. "It was she who set the fire. We must leave her with dignity."

"But he's getting away with her babies!"

"Let him go. He was never a Beast."

"But the babies are half Beast."

"Perhaps they will come back when they learn to know themselves."

* * * *

Icarus hugged me when I had finished the story. "Eunostos, we did come back! You got your babies again."

"Yes," I said, "and this time I mean to keep you." I looked at Thea and awaited the inevitable reprimand. She was certain to take her father's side, and already I was angry with her, remembering how she had laughed as that hateful man had carried her out of the forest.

At last, she said, "You can't blame him for leaving when he did. He was only thinking of us."

Icarus turned on her angrily. "But he left our mother."

"She always knew he would have to leave her," said Thea. But her eyes had filled with tears, and not, I guessed, for her father.

"Thea," I said. "I didn't—"

Pandia seized my hand. "There is someone watching us."

"A bear?" I smiled.

"Do bears wear helmets?"

Chapter VI

THE LOVE OF A QUEEN IS DEATH

The death which comes at the end of a long life, in a warm bed surrounded by loving children, is a lying down and not a darkness; it is not to be feared. But a slow and agonizing death in the fullness of youth is dreadful to men and dreaded even by gods. It was such a death which confronted the forest, though its rightful span was a thousand tearing winters and a thousand springs of healing violets and resurrecting roses.

No one knew at the time; no one knew that the death throes began when Pandia saw the helmet. How could a warrior have entered the forest, I asked, without being seen by the guards? No conch shell had blown to alert the Beasts. Perhaps, suggested Thea, Pandia had glimpsed a spying Paniscus and mistaken his horns for the boar's tusk of a helmet. Still, the mere possibility of Achaean infiltration left us with little appetite for the rest of our picnic. Returning to the Field of Gem Stones to recover our basket, we walked back to the house in thoughtful silence.

The following morning it was almost possible to forget the revelations and alarms of the preceding day. Breakfasting on bread, cheese, and carob pods, Thea did not refer to my unexpected embrace or to my story about her parents. She fed me some choice pods from her own plate and then withdrew to the shop to watch the Telchines cut some intaglios, while I remained in the garden, wondering what I should plant in place of my carrots. Perhaps a row of pumpkins, as big and friendly as the domestic pigs of the Centaurs. The day was benign; a blue monkey perched on the wall, waiting for Thea to feed him carrots. He would have a long wait.

Icarus emerged from the stairs. His hair was tousled from sleep and very long, rather like a nest in which baby mice have played. He had not yet donned a loincloth.

"Eunostos," he said. "I want to talk to you." Fifteen years sat lightly on his face, but the weight of a lifetime burdened his voice.

"You miss Perdix, don't you?" I said, trying to ease his very evident burden. The day before the picnic, he had suddenly announced that he had given Perdix his freedom—left him beside a carob tree in the forest. "To find a mate," was his sole explanation.

"No," he said. "Perdix was a child's pet. I am now a man." He used the word in the sense of a full-grown adult and not as a member of the human, as opposed to the bestial, race. We sat down on a stone bench in the shade of the parasol; splinters of sunlight jabbed through the crevices in the reds and pricked out shoulders. "Aren't I?"

"A man is strong," I said, "and strength makes him kind instead of tyrannical. A man is courageous, not because he lacks fear but because he conquers fear. Yes, Icarus, you are certainly a man, and one I am proud to call my brother."

"But that's not enough," he said impatiently. "Even if I were those things, which I doubt, I am still not manly in other ways. With women." His voice fell to a whisper, as if he ascribed to women the power and the mystery attributed to them in the days of stone implements, before it was known that the husband as well as the wife helped to produce a child. "I am—inexperienced."

I studied him carefully and saw that his body had hardened since he came to the forest; he was tanned and firm, with a down of hair on his cheeks, and I understood why Zoe had looked at him with desire as well as affection. Manliness mingled with innocence and cried to be awakened to knowledge of its own power.

"And you think I can help you?"

"I know you can. You and Zoe used to be more than friends, didn't you?"

I nodded, with perhaps a hint of a smirk.

"And other women too," he continued. "You must have had hundreds. You're just what they like. A regular bull of a man!"

Almost of itself, my chest expanded to its full dimensions, my tail twitched, my flanks felt the urge to strut.

"It's true that one kind likes me. Free-living women."

"One kind admits she likes you. Secretly, all of them do. Look at Thea."

The subject intrigued me. "Thea, you say?"

"Can't take her eyes off you. But frankly, the other, non-sisterly kind interests me more. I don't feel up to a long, exhausting courtship. I'm not as young as I was. That's why I want you to take me wenching."

"Wenching," I repeated, possibilities flickering through my brain like a covey of quail. "Suppose we call on Zoe and ask her to fetch you a young friend from the next tree."

"I don't like them young," he said with finality, "Experience, that's what I want. You see—" He paused in acute embarrassment. "I am not very practiced. The palace at Vathypetro limited my education. What does one talk about at such a time?"

"Compliments," I said. "One after another like pearls on a necklace. Give them something to wear—a bauble or an intimate garment such as a breast band—and then elaborate on how it becomes them. With my shop and workers, that's no problem. Jewels, sandals, whatever they like I've got."

"But you can't talk all the time," he said darkly. "Thea tried talking to Ajax when we were captives, but Ajax got tired of listening. He pushed her against the wall, and she had to use her pin. He wasn't a conversationalist, and neither am I."

"You'd be surprised how naturally the rest comes after the right gift and compliment. With the right woman, that is."

"The right woman. That's what I want you to help me find. And another thing. When I just think about wenching, I feel—well, a kind of fire creeping over my body. Arms. Chest. Stomach. Like a lizard with hot feet, if you know what I mean."

"The problem," I said, "is to find another lizard. We'll visit Zoe tomorrow. We'll ask her—"

"Eunostos! Icarus!" Thea called from the stairs.

"Later," I whispered in the conspiratorial tone of men discussing their favorite subject under grave risk of detection. "Here comes the watchdog."

"Eunostos, look at the intaglio I've cut!" she said, coruscating into the garden. She blazed in a lemon tunic which vied with the sun and gave her the look of a lithe young huntress; she had caught her hair in a knot behind her head and left her ears in piquant, pointed nakedness. I half expected a bow in her hand and a quiver at her back. Proudly she flaunted a large agate incised with the figure of a lion-haunched, eagle-headed griffin, the awesome but docile beast which the early Cretans had kept as pets in their palaces. "Where is Icarus? I wanted to show him too."

Icarus had left the garden. "I have no idea," I said, as convincingly as a bad liar can manage, though I had an idea of Icarus blithely making for a certain tree and a certain lady. The sly calf! He had wanted a woman of years and experience and no young friend from the next tree. I hoped that Zoe had told him the way.

"He shouldn't walk in the forest alone. If Pandia did see a warrior—"

"You can't keep him under foot all day. He isn't domestic, you know."

"No, I suppose not. He has seemed restless lately. Probably he needs a good walk in the forest to stir his blood. Call me when he returns, will you, Eunostos? I have to get back to the shop."

"Thea," I called after her. "Your ears—"

"Yes?" she smiled.

"Are very charming."

* * * *

Icarus, as he later explained, had gone to visit Zoe. Not knowing the way, he looked for Pandia to guide him. When he failed to attract her with calls and whistles, he hit on the plan of picking some blackberries which he ate or spilled as he walked. Pandia was not long in appearing to share the berries. No, she could not tell him the exact location of Zoe's tree—there were dozens of Dryads, after all—but she knew that it was close to some large beehives where she often gathered honey. She would lead him to the hives and perhaps they would meet someone who could give them further directions. She took his hand in case there were bears on the prowl.

"Your hand is sticky," he remarked.

"Oh," she said, "I missed some," licked her fingers to the last adhering seed, and reclaimed his hand. "You know," she resumed, "you ought to wear a loincloth."

"You think so?" said Icarus, flushing. In a hurry to leave the house, he had quite forgotten to dress.

"To hide your lack of a tail. It makes the back of you look lonesome." She moved to weightier subjects. "Are you going to have beer with Zoe?"

"Possibly," said Icarus. The thought occurred to him that the warm stimulus of beer might loosen his tongue and inspire him to dazzling compliments. Having come without a gift, he felt at a disadvantage.

"I wonder if she will have some cakes in the house."

"No," he said with authority. "She never keeps honey cakes. There is no need for you to go in for me. Or even wait." Secretly he hoped to linger with Zoe for several days, exploring the hidden tunnels and leafy porches and learning the harder steps of the Dance of the Python. He felt an unaccustomed and wholly exhilarating freedom. The voluptuous foretaste of manhood whetted his appetite like a roasted almond. He pictured Thea and Eunostos coming to Zoe's tree, and himself ensconced in a bark parapet and calling down to them: "Don't wait up for me. I'm spending the night."

They slithered through a thicket of bamboo, the slender, jointed canes as tall as their heads, the light green leaves rustling about their bodies like papyrus. Those consummate farmers, the Centaurs, said Pandia, in their ancient wandering, had imported the seeds from the Land of the Yellow Men.

Emerging from the thicket, they met a young man who seemed to be waiting for them. "You must be looking for my sister," he said. Icarus noticed the sickly softness of his flesh; he was not fat but he seemed without muscle, and his skin looked as if it would yield to the touch like the soft meat of a blowfish's belly. Otherwise, he was not unattractive: a golden down covered his arms and cheeks as if he had been dusted with pollen; his eyes were round and extraordinarily gold; and his tall wings were as black and pointed as the fin of a shark.

"Icarus, don't listen to him," hissed Pandia in a very audible whisper. "He is one of the Thriae. He may be planning to rob us."

"And what would I steal, your belt of rabbit's fur?" He smiled scornfully. "I am not stealing today, I am giving. Would you like to know what?"

Icarus did not intend to ask him. He resented the fellow's remark about Pandia's belt.

"What?" asked Pandia.

"Sisters," he said. "Or rather, one sister. Isn't that what you are looking for, Icarus? A man can recognize the look in another man's eyes. It says: I am tired of hunting and tired of gardening, of a man's work and the company of other men. I want soft lips and the teasing fragrance of myrrh, I want soft hands and the silken brush of hair."

"I am going to call on Zoe, the Dryad," said Icarus. (How, he wondered, had the young man learned his name?) "Do you know where she lives?"

"I know where everyone lives." He captured Icarus' arm and guided him through avenues of lofty carob trees, whose branches were freighted with pods like those which Thea had eaten for breakfast, while Pandia trailed behind them, peeling her eye in case the fellow should prove a thief after all and wish to steal her belt (or, horror of horrors, her pelt). Icarus, of course, had nothing to lose.

They stepped into a meadow riotous with flowers and murmurous with bees; flowers jabbing from the ground on pillar-straight stalks or undulating in green torrents of foliage; and bees which wavered above them like a black and golden nimbus and then exploded upward like sparks from a lightning-blasted tree and disclosed the cinnabar walls of black-hearted poppies, the lemon of green-backed gagea, the purpler-than-murex of hyacinths beloved by the gods. From just such a garden, thought Icarus, all the flowers of the earth, even the tame crocuses grown at Vathypetro, had come in the time before men, transported by bees and migratory birds and swift nomadic winds.

In the very midst of the flowers a vine-covered pole like the mast of a ship uplifted a light-seeming house with hexagonal walls of reeds, a thatched roof of dried water lily fronds, and opaque windows of waxed parchment. The first storm, you felt, would scatter the walls and collapse the roof. A summer house, hardly more enduring than flowers and hardly less beautiful: built to please and not to endure.

"Here," said the guide, "is the house."

"But Zoe lives in a tree."

"This is my sister's house."

Lifting aside a curtain of rushes, a young girl appeared in the door and looked down at Icarus with a confidence which seemed to say: "You will soon come up to me."

"Icarus," she chided. "You took your time in coming to call."

"How do you know my name? I don't know yours."

"The whole forest has heard about the handsome boy who has come to live with Eunostos, the Bull. And also about his sister, the very fastidious Thea, who keeps a watchful eye on both of her men. Does she know that her little brother is up to mischief?"

Icarus bristled. "It's no business of hers if I am."

"And what would she think of me? The wanton Amber, soliciting innocent boys."

"She would think you were very pretty." Indeed, she was smooth and bright as a tiger lily from the Land of the Yellow Men, with gold, violet-flecked eyes which did not change expression even when her lips curved to a smile, but looked like hungry mouths. When she spoke he saw that her tongue was long, thin, and freckled with gold like her eyes. She was even smaller than Thea. It should not be hard for her long wings to lift so small a body, thought Icarus. A winged lily she was, with catlike, sinuous grace; scarcely a girl at all except in the tightness she brought to her throat and the lizard with fiery feet she lashed across his limbs.

"Would you like to see my house?" she asked. "You will find it refreshing after your walk."

"I am going to call on Zoe," he repeated, with decidedly less enthusiasm than the first time he had made the announcement.

She laughed. "I think you are afraid of me. Of all women, perhaps, except little Bear Girls and blowsy old ladies like Zoe. Possibly you would prefer my brother. In the Cities of Men, I am told, the love of a man for a man is not uncommon. You will find it the same with drones like my brother. Among my people, the Thriae, queens like myself are rare and workers are no more excitable than a drudging mule. What can the poor drones do except console each other? They succeed rather well, I am told." She turned to her brother. "Does Icarus please you, my dear? He is succulent as a fig, and no bees, I think, have rifled his hive."

Her brother smiled and smiled; his golden tongue flicked between his moist lips and he did not need to speak.

"I've changed my mind," said Icarus to the girl. "How do I climb to your door?"

She lowered a ladder with rungs of cowhide. "When you've tasted my honey, you will feel as if you have wings. You will hardly need a ladder."

As he placed his foot in the first rung, Pandia caught at his arm. "I'm coming too."

"She hasn't any honey cakes, Pandia."

"She said honey, didn't she?"

"I think she meant hospitality."

The Bear Girl was close to tears. "It isn't really cakes I want. I don't want her to hurt you, that's all. She is a wicked woman. I can tell by the way she darts her tongue."

Laughter tinkled silvery about their heads. "Do you think me wicked, Icarus? Perhaps I am. How else would I know the thousand paths of pleasure?"

Hand over hand, his feet sinking in the hide of the rungs, Icarus climbed to the door. Amber gave him her hand and drew him over the threshold.

There were wicker chairs suspended from the ceiling on tenuous chains of grass. There were hangings of spider-spun silk through which the walls revealed their ribs of reed. Most of all, it was a room of flowers, which glowed in mounds like the heaped treasures spilled in Egyptian tombs when thieves are caught at their theft. One of the walls was coated with polished wax which mirrored the room like a misty garden and Amber's face as the queenliest of the blossoms. Surely, thought Icarus, no evil can touch me among so many flowers—there are even bees at work collecting nectar.

And yet the garden was captured; shut from the sunlight. He saw that Amber had quietly withdrawn the ladder.

"You have caught my friends at their trade." she smiled, pointing to the bees above a mound of jonquils. "Those are my workers. When the nectar enters their sacks, their bodily juices turn it into honey. Then they eject it into waxen trays and beat their wings to evaporate the water, leaving pure honey, which I in turn will trade for silks, jewels, and gold. Your own Eunostos has sometimes traded me bracelets. But you must not think that I also am a worker. I am a queen." She spoke the word with such impassioned pride that a crown seemed to glitter above her head and murex-colored robes tremble about her shoulders.

"What does a queen do?" He rather hoped that her answer would be mysterious and provocative. He was not disappointed.

"She lives like a flower, only for pleasure. For soft breezes and warm suns, the solicitations of butterfly and hawk moth, and all the sweet indolences of vegetable existence. But one pleasure is known to her which the flowers cannot comprehend."

He waited for her to reveal the name of this rarest pleasure.

"The gift of a man's embrace," she said at last, caressing the words as if they were priceless silk. "Shall I tell you the wealth of your own beauty? Number your masculine graces until a young god walks before the eye of your mind?"

"Would you?" he asked. He could not think of a more reassuring catalogue.

"A head of noble dimensions aureoled with luxuriant hair. A body swelling to manhood, the strong sinews of maturity asleep beneath the down of youth." She looked at him with a look between calculation and desire. "My dear, I am weary of butterflies. I crave the golden savagery of a bumblebee."

"I'm afraid," said Icarus, "that you want Eunostos instead of me. I think like a bumblebee, but I haven't learned how to buzz."

She seated him in one of the chairs suspended from the roof. She handed him a dish of pollen; she heated wine in a copper vessel over a small brazier and poured honey into the steaming liquid.

"Drink," she said. "Pleasure will stir in your veins even as the vine caresses your throat. Powerful wings will seem to beat at your shoulders."

He emptied the cup with one quick swallow. Was it a sudden breeze through the thin door of rushes? Was it the pounding of his own heart which swayed the chair into motion and disembodied him from the honeyed room and the weight of his limbs? Or did he move at all except in his mind?

She took his hand and steadied him onto his feet and led him inexorably to a mound of flowers. "Don't be afraid of crushing them," she said. "They have already yielded their gold, and now they are useless."

He felt as heavy as bronze. Insubstantiality had deserted him: reawareness of flesh, the imprint of stems against his bare body, and yes, the fiery feet of the lizard, assaulted his senses. Her hand touched his chest like a brand.

But her gold hypnotic eyes stared drowsiness into his limbs, and the sharp stems began to caress him like cool little tongues. He knew that he ought to crush her in his arms, possess her lips like a ravenous Ajax. Mimic the bumblebee and not the butterfly. But he seemed to be falling asleep. Zoe, he thought wistfully, Zoe aroused me to dance, but Amber puts me to sleep. Perhaps it is not I who am to blame.

Her face came toward him, a hungry golden moon, and swallowed him into the sky.

* * * *

The cowbell rang as peremptorily as if it had been returned to its cow. When I opened the door, Pandia clutched my hand. She had lost her belt and scuffed her sandals.

"That woman has got him in her hive," she whispered, as Thea appeared behind me.

"A Thria, you mean?" I gasped, incredulous, then comprehending. The queens were too diminutive to crave the embraces of Centaurs or Minotaur, and the small, hairy Panisci held no allurements for them. But a boy like Icarus—why had

I never thought to warn him? Why had I failed to answer his questions the day of the picnic?

"Yes. He climbed up the ladder and sent me away."

"Show us the house," cried Thea, and Pandia gulped some air and gamely trotted ahead of us.

The house loomed above our heads, as closed and apparently inaccessible as a tortoise shut in its shell. The girl had withdrawn the ladder, the doors and windows were latched. But for once my height proved a boon. I grasped the narrow ledge in front of the door and drew myself onto the sill. Flinging aside the curtain of rushes, I burst into the room. The sweetness hit me like syrup flung from a cup; at once it teased and sickened. The murmuring bees sounded like flies as they buzz around a dead body. I saw the ladder coiled inside the door, and I saw Icarus, pale as foam, in the Thria's arms.

I lunged through mounds of flowers; the bees scattered before me, roaring, and returned to sting my legs. I did not feel them. I seized the girl by the wings and tore her off my friend as one tears a crab away from a stricken fish. She whimpered but did not fight me. There was something loathsome and predatory about her; or worse, scavenging, for she lacked the bold courage of the predator. She preyed on helpless boys.

"It is too late." She smiled. "I have breathed death into his lungs."

"Lower the ladder," I gasped with a voice which was frozen between rage and anguish. She moved toward the door. I saw that she meant to escape. I sprang between her and the door and threw the ladder to Thea and Pandia.

"Watch her," I said as they climbed into the room.

When Thea saw Icarus, she paled and held back a cry, but she did not wallow in useless hysterics. To Amber she said:

"Help my brother, or I will tear the wings from your back."

"There is only one way to help him," I said. "I must try to draw the poison from his lungs."

"Let me," said Thea. It was not composure she showed, which implies a want of feeling, but courage wrestled from fear. She had hated and feared the forest; now she was facing its most insidious threat without dismay. "Let me, Eunostos. He is my brother."

"And my friend," I said.

"It may prove fatal to you?"

"Yes." I pressed my mouth to his colorless lips. Like a hunter drawing the venom from the bite of a snake, I sucked the air which Amber had breathed from her noxious lungs. It did not burn, but entered my throat insidiously like a thick oozing of honey.

How suddenly small he seemed, how limp and white and seemingly lifeless! The yearning came to me that he should be my son by Thea: I kissed her, kissing him, and then we laughed through the forest, each of us holding his hand. Now he was a small boy with a large head, and now an infant swinging on our arms, the child I had loved in Kora's tree-house. Icarus, Icarus, my son, breathe your poison into my lungs, for I am like your father, and a father's part is to guard his son from the Striges of the night and the Ambers of the day; to take the arrow intended for his vulnerable breast, the flung stone, the rending claw. What is love but a shield of hammered bronze?

My head fell against his cheek, and sleep possessed me like a falling of leaves…

Daylight flooded the room. I saw that Thea had taken my place with Icarus; first, she must have broken the parchment out of the windows and flooded the room with light and air.

"Thea," I whispered. "Now we have both been poisoned."

"Divided the poison," she said. "That is the difference."

Icarus opened his eyes and spoke sleepily. "There was honey in my lungs. It was very sweet. It made me want to sleep." Like a child in a warm bed with stuffed animals, he drew us close to him.

"You mustn't sleep now," I said. "There is still poison in your body." I helped him to his feet. He took a faltering step, caught my arm, and managed to cross the room without help.

"I am ready now," he said.

Thea watched him with pride, as if he were learning to walk for the first time. No sooner had he crossed the room, however, than she flung an accusing question:

"Icarus, why did you come to this house?"

He spoke without apology. "I was going to call on Zoe. I lost my way."

She flared like a pine-knot torch. "Your friend, Eunostos. He was going to see your friend! You sent him to her, didn't you?"

"No," I said, "but I intended to take him myself the next day."

"You wanted to lie with her. Both of you. To lie with a harlot."

Harlot indeed! Zoe, the kindest of women. Anger made me eloquent, and also cruel. "She is warm, generous, and womanly. It's true that she gives her body. But you give nothing. Your body has no more warmth than a drift of snow. I was happy until you came. I had my friends, my house, and my garden, and no one asked me to behave like a eunuch. What did you do? Despised my friends, changed my house, and picked my flowers. Zoe is better than you, in spite of her lovers. She at least is a woman and you are a bloodless prude."

She slapped me across the mouth before I had time to regret my accusation. I shoved her onto the floor. She fell with a startled gasp and sat in a mound of poppies like an image of the Great Mother on a throne of flowers, but without the Mother's composure.

"Icarus," she wailed, as if to say: "Give me a hand and take your sister's part against this brute."

But Icarus let her sit. "We are still going to call on Zoe," he said.

"Watch the bee woman," warned Pandia. "She's up to something."

Exchanging accusations, we had quite forgotten the cause of our quarrel. Pandia had been more vigilant.

"I've kept an eye on her," she said. She had taken a stance at the door with fire tongs in her hand. "If she had tried to get by me, I would have let her have it. But she's starting to cry, and that must mean a trick."

Indeed, Amber had crouched among her now beeless flowers, and silent tears had diamonded her cheeks.

Icarus went to her side. "We are not going to hurt you."

"You think I am weeping from fear?"

"Remorse then?" I asked. "Isn't it a little late?"

"I am weeping for myself," she said, "and my own pitiless heart. He lay in my arms, frightened and gentle—a boy's innocence and a man's body. Intimately loveable, infinitely pitiable. Yet I could not love him. I could not pity him. And so, when I saw the three of you hurling the anger which is another face of love, I wept for envy. I wept my first and my last tears. I live in a house of flowers, but I pick them only for their honey and never regret the crushed petal or the broken stem. I will always be a seeker of honey, it seems. The honey of flowers—or gold."

"Gold?" I asked with suspicion. "Someone paid you, didn't he? It was not your wish to love which made you seek out Icarus. You were paid to kill him with your kisses!"

She began to laugh. "What will you pay me to learn who paid me?"

"Your life."

She looked at my knotted fist and powerful hooves. "Achaeans. As they paid the rest of my people. We have let some of their scouts enter the forest."

"The man called Ajax?" cried Thea. "Was he among them?"

"Yes. He has given us bracelets and offered a tortoise shell full of gold to the one who kills or betrays you into his hand. You, Icarus, and Eunostos. To get you, he will even launch an invasion."

Chapter VII

INVASION

We reached the lands of the Centaurs shortly before twilight. Moschus and his countrymen were fighters as well as farmers, the strongest of the six tribes of Beast, and their leader Chiron was the uncrowned king of the forest. We were coming to tell them about the treachery of the Thriae. In times of peace, each of the tribes retained and jealously guarded its independence, but in times of danger everyone looked to Chiron: for example, the cold winter when the wolves came down the mountains to steal our game and children. "Dip your arrows in the juice of the wolf's-bane root," suggested Chiron. We routed the wolves with our first charge, and Moschus acquired his sash.

We crossed an irrigation ditch and entered a trellised vineyard where little kernels, green and hard like sea grapes, would sweeten and purple with approaching summer until they lured the bees even from the houses of the Thriae; an olive grove whose silver leaves had tarnished with the dying sun to the fitful sheen of old jewelry; and then a grove of palm trees imported from Libya and nurtured to the date-clustered, full-branched opulence of a desert oasis. Next, we skirted the enclosed compound of the cattle, whose fence of sharpened stakes withheld nocturnal bears and the occasional hardy wolf which still descended from the mountains, and came to the wall-less town of the Centaurs.

I walked to the edge of the moat and peered at the sharpened stakes which bristled from its depths like the teeth of a barracuda. A surer defense than walls, I thought with a shudder. And yet the shrewd Achaeans were not likely to balk at such an obstacle. I knew of their battering rams which, if two were placed end to end, could erect a narrow bridge, and I noticed a clump of olive trees dangerously close to the moat and offering cover to an enemy wishing to cross in the dead of night.

"Chiron," I boomed, and the tallest and kingliest of all the Centaurs detached himself from his friends and galloped toward us along a path which was strewn with seashells.

"Eunostos," he neighed, rearing to a halt on the other side of the moat. "We don't hear that bellow often enough. And I see you've brought your new friends, and little Pandia, hungry no doubt." He entered a low wooden tower with a flat roof, and presently a narrow, railed drawbridge, supported by bronze chains, eased over the moat with the soundlessness of a great eagle descending from the sky (it was one of my own designs). We met at the bridge and I told him about the Thriae.

His face darkened. "I am not surprised. They are capable of any mischief. We will have to take steps."

We followed him into the town. His mane seemed a drift of snow, newly fallen and not yet hard, and his wide, unblinking eyes held the blue clarity of a lake in the Misty Isles on one of those rare days without mist. His eyes saw everything; they could hold anger but never rancor. They understood and sometimes even judged, but they never condemned. He was not an ascetic, you understand. Those who live close to the soil like the Centaurs, growing crops and raising cattle, always keep something of earth in their veins and in their faces. They are farmers and not philosophers. But earth in Chiron had been purified to the white, finely sifted sand of a coral beach.

The bamboo stalls of the Centaurs were twinkling on their lights. They were long, slender houses built of bamboo, with pointed roofs and open ends, and above each threshold hung a lamp enclosed in an orange parchment and called a "lantern" and a small wicker cage which held a humming cricket, the luck of the house (remember, the Centaurs had traveled to the

Land of the Yellow Men). At night the Centaurs slept on their feet, leaning against the wall, which they covered with silken tapestries from the looms of the Dryads to ease their sensitive flanks, and resting their hooves in a carpet of clover, renewed each morning by the diligent females while their husbands worked in the fields.

Some of the males were bathing in terracotta tubs adapted to their long frames and ending with a trough in which they could rest their arms and head. They snorted and flailed their legs and kicked water at friends who happened to pass within their range. The females were building fires in front of the houses or cleaning the hoes and rakes which the males had brought from the fields or feeding the small, plump, and immaculate pigs which they kept for pets as Men kept dogs or monkeys. My good friend Moschus erupted from one of the tubs and, lathered with konia, a cleansing lye with a base of ashes, cantered to greet us. He nodded curtly to Thea, paternally to Icarus, and seized both my hands. Before he could hint for an invitation, Chiron told him our news.

"Blow the conch, will you, Moschus?" he asked. "It is time for a conclave."

Moschus blew the conch as forcefully as he blew the flute, and an oceanic summons compounded of many sounds—the indrawing tide, the foaming disintegration of waves as they met the beach, the bodiless wails of drowned mariners—boomed implacably across the land. The Centaurs dropped their tools, forsook their baths, and, accompanied by their pigs, followed us to the theatrical area in the center of town, a round pit open to the sky, circled with flaring torches, and ringed with twelve stone tiers of seats. It was here that they performed their dramas in honor of the Great Mother, whom they call the Corn Goddess, and her son, the Divine Child, and raised their resonant voices in dithyrambs of praise.

After the Centaurs came the other Beasts: the Panisci from their burrows, annoyed at being summoned before they had stolen their supper; the Bears of Artemis, who, roused from their hollow logs, were rubbing their eyes sleepily and combing their fur with combs of tortoise shell; the Dryads, tall and beautiful like their trees and redolent of bark and tender buds of spring. And of course the Thriae, ignorant, it seemed, of Amber's betrayal. They fluttered out of the sky in three swarms: the drones with busy titterings and quick feminine jerks of their wings; the workers dour, unsmiling, and heavy of movement, as if encased in armor; and last, three of the queens (Amber, the fourth, did not appear) with their dignity somewhat lessened by the heavy gold bracelets jangling on their arms.

Chiron, lord of the Centaurs, descended the twelve stone tiers and entered the pit. No sooner had he raised his noble head than silence enveloped his audience. You could hear the bleat of a sheep in the compound of the animals, and close at hand, the peremptory squeal of a pig, whose master silenced him with a thump to his tail.

Chiron spoke. His words had the ringing urgency of a trumpet blast. "Grave charges have been made. Grave warnings offered. We will hear from Eunostos, our esteemed friend."

Rustic that I am, gardener and artisan, I have no skill at oratory (though perhaps a modicum as a poet), and the sullen crowd dismayed me. Summoned without explanation, they poised rather than sat and waited to be cajoled and convinced—except for my friends, who stood on the edge of the pit. Thea was smiling encouragement; extending her little hand in a gesture of affection and support. Pandia was trying her best to look attentive and conceal the fact that she would rather eat supper than listen to a speech. Icarus looked—well, worshipful. Whatever I said would sound inspired to him.

I spoke: "Ever since we came to the forest to escape the harassment of Men, we have lived in peace and abundance. Each of us has worked in his own way to make his own contribution. Each of us has done what the Great Mother designed him to do. Our hosts, the Centaurs, have supplied us with produce from their well cultivated farms. The Dryads have woven silk on the looms in their trees. The Thriae, the Bears of Artemis, the Panisci—need I remind you of their skill and their dedication?" (It was also unnecessary, I felt, to remind them that the Thriae had always made good thieves as well as workers). "In the past, we have been content to live to ourselves. Self-completeness has been our aim and our achievement. No longer. One of our tribes has hungered for foreign gold."

I paused, not for dramatic effect like a Centaur reciting a dithyramb, but to catch my breath and find the words for my peroration. I had caught their interest. Now I must goad them to action.

I pointed my finger at the queens of the Thriae.

"There stand the guilty Beasts—traders for gold and traitors to our people. I have it from the mouth of their fourth queen that she and her people have accepted gold to betray my friends into the hands of the Achaeans. To gain this end, they have promised to help the Achaeans invade the forest."

INVASION! An audible gasp, incredulous, hushed, rippled along the tiers like a wind in the boughs of a palm tree. Such was the fear which our bestial characteristics—horns, hooves, tails—had inspired among Men, such was our isolation among the mountains, that invasion had never threatened us in all the years since the Beasts had come to the forest. Only Aeacus, by our own sufferance, had strayed among our fastnesses and returned to Knossos with tales or silences to strengthen our legend. Nevertheless, Chiron and other elderly beasts remembered the time when we had lived near the sea and pirates had landed in Gorgon-prowed ships to burn our farms and capture slaves. Remembered the splintering doors, the red dragons of fire constricting their coils around our reed-build houses, the cries of infant Panisci caught in nets and Dryads dragged by their hair through burning olive groves… the haughty sneer of the Cretan king when those who survived the attack demanded justice: "Protect your own. I am not responsible for the chance attack of pirates." …The final agonizing decision to retreat to the safety of the forest and forsake the Men with whom we had lived in harmony for many centuries…the angry farmers, reluctant to lose our help in the fields, trying to stop us and Chiron confronting them with a terrible ultimatum: "Prevent our flight and Blue Magic will destroy your crops." … Centaurs burning the fields at night with a cloud of fertilizer…blackened vines in place of luxuriant vineyards and terrified farmers urging us on our way with gifts of milk and cheese and all the while exalting us into Legend, not Men, not Beasts, but four-legged, cloven-hoofed demons who could blight the crops with their evil, witching eyes…

Chiron advanced to the edge of the pit and leveled a steely gaze at the three queens. "What is your answer to these charges brought by Eunostos?"

One of the queens, the oldest, made her way down the tiers and occupied the pit as if it were a throne. A wizened woman, with mottled skin and huge golden eyes, she had hidden her arms with bracelets which clattered when she walked.

Her voice was honey and salt. "His human friends have bewitched our good Eunostos. Whatever plot is afoot, it is they—the girl and her brother—who have perpetrated it, and we poor Thriae are its victims. I know of no gold from Achaean soldiers, unless it has gone to the witch-child Thea and her big-headed brother."

"And this?" I asked, pointing to a bracelet strung with miniatures of the death masks worn by Mycenaean kings. "Did you get this from my shop?"

She looked at her wrist. "Where else? Your workers traded it to me for six jars of honey."

"No Telchin made it," I said. "In my shop or anywhere else in the forest. They can only copy what they have seen. Death masks belong to Mycenae and Tiryns."

She shrugged. The Thriae are quick to lie and brazen when they are caught. Her wings unruffled, she said: "Suppose it is true that we accepted a few Achaean bracelets in return for the human children. If we let your Thea and Icarus stay in the forest, they will surely bring evil down on us as their father did. Need I remind you that their mother, Kora, was burned to death in her tree? My people and I merely wish to see these dangerous intruders driven from our midst. We did not conspire to see the forest invaded. If you do fear invasion, I suggest you deliver the children to us, and we in turn will give them to the Achaeans and remove all threat."

"She calls us the human children," protested Icarus. His voice was strong and compelling. "She does us a terrible wrong. By her own admission, our mother was the Dryad Kora. Look at my ears and tell me I am a Man!"

"Keep the children! They belong here as surely as I do." It was Zoe. I wanted to hug her.

And Moschus: "Keep the children!"

"KEEP THE CHILDREN!"

Welling from a hundred throats, the plea had become a command, sharp, imperious, not to be denied. The old queen fluttered her bulging eyes, but Chiron silenced her before she could speak.

"Keep them we will. Defend them we will against invaders. And you," he blazed at the queen, "you and your people are no longer welcome at our counsels or in our forest. Go to the men who have bought you with gold. Tell them that they attack us at their risk."

The queen smiled and her thick lips writhed like a jellyfish. "Have you shields to withstand the bite of their axes?" she asked. "Have you greaves and breastplates and helmets? I think we will soon be returning with the conquerors. Fatten your pigs to feast us when we come."

The Centaurs closed their hooves protectively around their pigs and shrank from the opening wings of the drones, who, tittering nervously, kicked themselves from the ground with a decorous lilt of their toes. The workers lumbered after them, their customary sullenness darkened to a glowering rage, and the three proud queens ascended the sky as if they were climbing the stairs of a palace and extinguished themselves in the labyrinth of night.

Chapter VIII

THE BULL THAT WALKS
LIKE A MAN

In the time preceding a battle, the trivialities of peace become eloquent. The lamplit roots of my den, twisting their friendly protection above our heads, seemed to say: Enjoy while you can the pungent musk of scrambled woodpecker eggs and the amber conviviality of beer poured from a skin. Tastes sharpen, colors intensify, and love, like a friendly ancestral serpent, leaves a beneficent trail across the floor. Thea and I had fought each other in the house of Amber: with blows and crueler words. But no one alluded now to our differences. After the war, we could speak again of the old anger and the old pride and admit, perhaps, that each had needed to speak yet spoken too much. But now, in the forest's last tranquility, I knew that I loved her with all the ardors of my once fickle heart. It is said that the Great Mother was formerly a maiden, slender and virginal, who lived in a house of willow boughs where all the animals came to bring her food and lay their horns and antlers beneath her hands. Willingly would I have laid my tangled mane beneath my Thea's hand. She did not touch me, but sometimes her hand trembled in the air between us, as if with the least encouragement it would come to rest like a tired butterfly. Shyness held me from touching her, and the fear that, once having touched, I would love her to my despair and perhaps destruction.

Every morning we met in my shop. Icarus whittled arrows from the boughs of linden trees and Thea fitted them with heads of flint, sharpened to lethal points. My workers and I were hammering a shield for Icarus.

"I ought to surrender," said Thea. "It's me they want, much more than you and Icarus. It was I who angered Ajax—hurt his pride. If I went to him now, he might forget his invasion."

"He's a warrior," I said, "with a taste for battle. Any battle. His hurt pride is merely an excuse for launching him on a new adventure. Achaeans are always getting their pride hurt to give them a pretext for war. They hold it over their heads like a parasol and rattle their swords when it catches a few raindrops. Even if you went to him, he would still attack us. In addition to our gold, we're worth a fortune as slaves. It's been a long time since Panisci performed in the court of Egypt."

"And a Minotaur," said Icarus. "They would probably send you to pleasure the queen. I expect you would bring two fortunes. Much more than my sister."

"And," I continued quickly to Thea, "even if you could stop the war, I wouldn't let you go to him. I don't mean to let you out of the forest again."

"I have no wish to leave." She touched my hand at last. "What are our chances, Eunostos? I have seen those dreadful Achaeans. Their only love is to fight. They are brutally strong and foolishly brave and so girded with armor—greaves, cuirasses, helmets—that their flesh is almost unassailable."

"The Centaurs also are stout fighters," I said. "Farming keeps them in shape. Being both horse and rider, they surpass the best cavalry. They can charge like the wind, grapple with their hands, and kick with their hooves."

"But numbers are against us, I think. How many Centaurs are there?"

"Forty males."

"There must be a hundred Achaeans with Ajax, and all of them armed to the teeth. The Centaurs have only their clubs and their bows and arrows."

"Don't forget the Panisci, and don't mistake them all for children. Some are middle-aged and very wily. There must be fifty of them." (They were much too furtive for an exact count.)

"And how many Thriae?"

"Fifty, but some are drones and of little account. The queens, I suspect, will guide the Achaeans and show them every secret turning in the forest. There will be no chance for us to lay an ambush, except in the deeply wooded sections where the Thriae can't fly."

"But we have you," said Icarus proudly. "You're worth an army of Achaeans. I am going to fight at your side."

"In time you will," I said. "In time we will fight together like two old comrades. For the moment, however, I want you to stay with Thea and the Telchines to store supplies and guard the house. If the Centaurs and I should lose the first battle, I will need a place in which to lick my wounds, and as you know, this tree is as good as a fort."

He sighed heavily but did not protest the disagreeable order. Truly, I thought, he is learning to be a warrior.

"I will guard your house," he said, "and keep it safe."

"Now look at the shield my workers have made for you!" I said, touched by his vow. Shaped like a figure eight, embossed with luck-bringing serpents inspired by Perdix, it was such a shield as kings have borne into battle to give their names to legend. Accepting the gift from Bion's two front legs, Icarus held it at arm's length and waved his free arm as if to brandish a sword.

"Ho," he cried, "ho," as he stepped and lunged, parried and ducked, pretending to run me through the chest. Then he remembered to thank the Telchin. He patted his head. "It is very beautiful." The Telchin was not impressed. "It is quite the most fearful and deadly shield I have ever seen!" he continued. "It will help me to slay a dozen warriors, and mingle their blood with its golden snakes. I will name it for you. I will name it Bion."

The Telchin bobbed his head in wordless devotion.

It was Pandia who came to tell us that Chiron had blown the conch shell to assemble his army against the Achaeans.

* * * *

They marched across the field in ragged but resolute lines, their leather boots tearing the yellow gagea and cracking the willow rods of our fallen glider. They moved toward the trees like walking flames, yellow of armor, its bronze enkindled by sunlight; yellow of beard below their crested, sunbright helmets. The queens of the Thriae, Amber among them, circled busily above the soldiers. The sullen workers had yet to make their appearance, but the drones were dimly visible on the far side of the field, beyond the range of our arrows but close enough for their animated chatter to reach us like a distant droning of bees.

We lurked in the trees, and clumsy shields of cow's hide, hurriedly made by the Centaurs in our few days of grace, lay at our feet like the belts of animals. At Chiron's signal we stepped between the trunks, aimed with unhurried precision, and loosed a volley of arrows. The queens of the Thriaes shot above the threatening shafts. They shook their fists and their sweet voices piped incongruous oaths; Amber, the youngest, was also the loudest in her denunciation of the "foul horses" and the "rutting Minotaur". The hundred Achaeans fell to their knees in a ring and raised their broad round shields above their heads. They resembled a giant tortoise, and our well-aimed arrows fell noisily but harmlessly onto their collective shell. Again, the creak of the linden bow, the twang of the arrow guided with the green tail feathers of a woodpecker. Again, the stout, resistant shell. Six times we drew and loosed our arrows. At last a few of them began to penetrate the crevices between the shields, and one of the shields, two, three collapsed as if a giant invisible foot had stepped on the tortoise and broken a part of its shell. But our quivers would soon be emptied.

"Enough," said Chiron. "Let them advance. We will fight them among the trees."

Once among the trees, they had to advance in narrow files, and the branches above their heads were so heavy with vines that the Thriae could not guide them and point out our hidden presences. But arrows were useless in such terrain and among the close-set trees the long Centaurs and a tall Minotaur were limited in their prowess. Here, the best fighters were the sly, agile Panisci. Their little hairy bodies could blend with the vegetation. They could crawl where Centaurs could not walk: retreat, advance, circle, harass with their bruising slings. They fired at the areas of flesh which were not protected by armor—the face—the arms, the thighs. Their stones moved so quickly that they might be mistaken for large, soundless insects; they were no less painful for the fact that they disabled instead of killed.

Cries of astonishment greeted the first barrage. Men clapped hands against their wounded flesh and drew them away when their fingers oozed with blood.

"It's children," squealed Ajax (I knew him from Thea's description). "They've sent their children against us!"

"Children, Hades," cried Xanthus, the one who had lost his ears. "It's goats!" He lunged at a flying hoof and received a blow to his chin. "And watch those hooves!"

One of the Achaeans, harassed out of his line by the slingers, leaned on the trunk of an oak to catch his breath. A faint groaning of wood alerted him to scan the leaf-shrouded limbs. Did the rascally slingers—children, goats, demons, whatever they were—hide in trees? A noose-shaped vine tightened around his neck and jerked him from his feet. He kicked and waved his arms; he could not scream. The friends who cut him down discovered a corpse who had bitten through his tongue. Above their heads, a woman's laughter tinkled among the branches; her green hair was indistinguishable from the leaves.

But furtive slingers and gallant Dryads could not be expected to stop the Achaean advance. Only Centaurs and I could hope for decisive victory, and not among trees but in the first clearing. We watched them stagger with slain or wounded comrades into the open grasses and imbibe courage from the bountiful sun. We counted their losses: three we had killed with arrows; four had been stunned by the slings of the Panisci; and three had been hanged by Dryads. It was time for the Centaurs and me.

By choice I am not a fighter, but a worker of gems and metals, a sometime gardener, a peace-loving rustic, and finally a poet. But who can follow a trade or write a poem when helmeted warriors are stomping about the country and threatening to ravish the women? The time to fight is not the time to garden, and no Beast should hesitate to exchange his hoe for a sword. I preferred the hoe. On the other hand, I did not fear the sword.

"Despoilers of women," I thundered. "Burners, looters, pillagers, and Zeus-damned Northerners!"

The Achaeans awaited our charge with stupefaction. Their mouths dropped open as if they had broken their jaws, and their blue eyes widened to utter vacuity. Well, perhaps they had reason to blanch. Forty thundering Centaurs can raise more clatter than a hundred horse-drawn chariots. Then I saw the cause of their dread was not the Centaurs. It was me. The Minotaur. *The Bull That Walks Like a Man*. They scattered before my advance like chickens surprised by a wolf. They risked the multiple hooves of Moschus or Chiron to escape the mere two arms of a Minotaur. No sooner had I swung my axe than I found myself swinging at empty air. One of them, two, I laid on the ground with well-aimed blows, but the others kept out of reach. Enough. I did not intend to tire myself in futile pursuit.

"Ajax," I boomed. "In the name of the Princess Thea, I challenge you to mortal combat!"

No true warrior, least of all a battle-loving Achaean, can ignore a personal challenge, and Ajax, in spite of his ignorance, lechery, and dirt, was not a coward. He lost no time in answering my summons, though I cannot say that he exactly charged me; rather, he squeaked: "Minotaur, here I am!" and tensed himself to receive my blows.

Somewhat doubtfully protected by my shield of cow's hide, I charged him with the anything but doubtful deadliness of my double-headed axe, its bronze blade smelted and sharpened in my own shop. My battle-axe was much less wieldy than Ajax's sword, but much more deadly if I landed a blow. You never jab with an axe like a fisherman spearing fish—you swing and slash in great half-circles, from side to side or head to foot. He jabbed, withdrawing: I swung, advancing. When his potent shield deflected my blows, I discarded my useless framework of hide and pressed him with such abandon that he dropped his shield and clutched the hilt of his sword with both of his hands. The muscles which Thea had once admired in my arms tautened to the struggle; leaped beneath my skin like the slashing jaws of a crab. You know, I am clumsy when I walk in the house. I stumble on carpets and trip on stairs. I overturn pitchers of wine and spill bones in my lap. But a furious rhythm directed me as I lunged and parried, lunged and parried, gaining a foot, holding my ground, gaining, holding, gaining. The clash of metal became a martial music which stirred my feet, my hands, my torso to the long exhilarating dance of war. And Ajax started to tire. He blinked the sweat from his hairybrowed eyes; he gasped like a diver wrestling an octopus.

"Xanthus," he called at last. "Pluton, help me!" and two of his cohorts, battling a wounded Centaur, leaped to defend their chief. Two, mind you! Three men against one Minotaur. I swung my axe in a rapid, deadly circle. But the earless Xanthus used his sword like a spear and threw it at my legs. It slashed me above the ankle. I gave such a roar that a momentary silence settled across the field; Achaeans and Centaurs poised between their blows and stared at me with gleeful or sorrowful eyes; awaited the fall of the Beast which had walked like a Man.

While Xanthus recovered his sword, Ajax and Pluton pressed their attack. They thought, no doubt, to find me lamed and helpless. But my roar had vented anger and not defeat. The side of my axe bit into Pluton's neck; in the handle, I felt the spasms of his death-struck body. I had not time in which to recover my axe. Ajax came at me with murder in his hand. He looked like a hungry sphinx. The stench of him struck me in the face.

"Ajax," I railed. "You ought to take a bath." I lowered my horns and butted him off his feet.

Then I heard Chiron's cry: "Withdraw, withdraw to the woods!"

Withdraw? Unthinkable! Had not my forefathers said: "Never turn tail until you have lost your horns?"

But I saw the reason behind the command. A second army had entered the field.

Chapter IX

ARROWS AND HONEY

A hundred fresh Achaeans had entered the field. Probably Ajax had lured them from the coast with promises of gold and slaves: Centaurs to draw their chariots; Panisci to sell in the marketplace at Pylos. Our retreat was rapid but not disorganized. We left behind us five dead Centaurs, their limbs awry in the grim ungainliness of death, and yet their eyes still open and seemingly as sentient as when they had scanned a new network of irrigation ditches or studied the secrets of the Yellow Men. Fortunately, the reinforcing Achaeans did not follow us into the trees; they seemed content to succor their battered comrades, who had lost a fifth of their numbers to hooves and battle-axes.

"We shall go to defend our town," said Chiron, when a grove of carob trees had separated us from the hateful field. "Eunostos, why don't you get your friends and join us? We have enough food to withstand a long siege. Remember how we beat off the wolves for three whole weeks?"

"You might bring us a few skins of beer," whispered Moschus, who followed close on my tail.

"If I stay in my house," I explained, "we will make the Achaeans divide their strength. Small as it is, it can stand a siege." I could not admit that I doubted the strength of their town, in spite of its bristling moat.

"Do as you please," said Chiron, though Moschus audibly grumbled. "I hope your little friends can draw a bow."

"They are both good fighters. And of course they blame themselves for the war. Thea offered to surrender herself to Ajax."

"Not a bad idea," muttered Moschus, but Chiron silenced him with a glare.

"Tell them they aren't to blame. Sooner or later, Men were bound to attack us. We are too unlike them—our hearts as well as our bodies. Nature to us is sometimes irascible, sometimes unpredictable, but still—a friend. To them, in spite of all their talk about worshiping the Great Mother, she is either a slave or a master. They fear her unless they can put her in chains."

I traveled home by way of Pandia's house. Her town was undefended, and I wanted to offer her asylum in my trunk. It was not really a town; a hamlet, no more, with a dozen hollowed logs placed in a ring around a carefully cultivated berry patch—blackberries for food, bearberries for a bracing, astringent drink. The patch was crisscrossed with narrow paths and thickly quilled with posts where baskets of berries could be hung on wooden hooks. The open ends of the logs confronted the patch and allowed the owners to keep a watchful eye for the stealthy crows which came with twilight.

I crossed the crooked stream which carried snow from the mountains and laved the town in a cool, perpetual breeze. No one greeted me; no one contested my approach. I paused at a low, thorn-rimmed fence and raised the latch of the gate with as much noise as possible to announce my arrival. The back ends of the logs, sealed with clay and stained with umber, stared at me like lidless eyes. I walked between two of the logs and emerged within the circle and facing the front doors. Each log was high enough to enclose two rooms, their rounded walls hewn and polished to a smooth finish. The first room served as a pantry, whose open shelves abounded with jars of honey and bowls of berries, and also with trays of freshly smoked fish, a little rank to the nostrils of a Minotaur. The second room, invisible behind a curtain of dried black-eyed Susans strung on silken strands, I knew to be the sleeping quarters or, in the term of the Girls, the Repositorium. One of the Girls was moving drowsily through the berry patch and filling a pail which hung from her paw.

"Where is Pandia?" I asked without polite preliminaries.

She pointed to one of the logs. "Asleep. It's the Afternoon Repose, you know. I was sleeping too till I dreamed about dinner."

Stooping to half my normal height, I entered the arch of the designated house, flung aside the curtain of black-eyed Susans, and found Pandia asleep beneath a coverlet of rabbit skins, with a pot of Cretan Bears-tail twisting its yellow and purple flowers on a table beside her couch.

"Pandia?" I called. "PANDIA." She did not stir.

"Bears," I said.

She threw back the coverlet and almost overturned the pot of flowers. "Bears?"

"Human bears; Achaeans. They have won the first battle and entered the forest. Would you like to come to my house and stay with Icarus and me?"

"Yes."

"Would your friends like to visit the Centaurs? They would be much safer there."

"We don't like the pigs. Besides," she added, "the Achaeans may not bother us. There is nothing here they could want."

She neatened her hair with a comb of tortoise shell, hurriedly tied her rabbit sash in a bow with unequal ends, and followed me out of the village with one regretful look at the berry patch.

"Do you know what war is?" She sighed. "It's giving up berries so you can stick swords in people."

"But if we don't give up the berries, we shall have to lose Thea and Icarus."

"You're right," she admitted, "and Icarus is worth a whole patch. He's rather like berries himself, you know. Good to have at the table or in the kitchen, sweet but not sugary. Except he doesn't have thorns."

"He's learning to grow them. He must."

We jogged through the forest on rapid, silent feet. I always lower my horns when spurred by danger, an instinctive reaction, no doubt, to shield myself with the fiercest part of me. Crippled as I was by a sword-slashed ankle, Pandia matched my pace and sometimes spurted ahead of me in her eagerness to join Icarus. Her nub of a tail quivered with fear and excitement.

I felt an enormous relief when I saw my house, its friendly brown ramparts lifting an island in the afternoon. Then I stopped. The house was beleaguered by Thriae! A dozen of the dour workers, conspicuously absent before the battle, were wheeling above the trunk with dulcet cries of "Drown Icarus" and "Burn Thea" (you would rather expect them to boom like warring generals, but even the workers have honeyed voices). Arrows whirred from the trunk like the green woodpeckers whose feathers guided their shafts. One of the Thriae stiffened in the midst of a cry and fell from the air as if she had turned to stone. Good. Thea and Icarus were manning the parapet. But how could I reach the door with my lamed ankle?

"Pandia, do you want to go back to your village? You may be safer there."

"Not while those Harpies are after Icarus."

I lifted her in my arms, bending to shield her body, and entered the deadly field. We had covered a third of the distance to the trunk when the Thriae saw us. Like geese in the shape of a wedge, they wheeled to attack us with a shower of rocks, which they carried in quivers at their sides and hurled with deft jabs of their hands. The drone of their wings made a low, continuous thunder. The rocks were small but jaggedly cutting. My large, bowed back made an excellent target, and so did the fiery thatch of my head. For once I was glad of my matted hair, which doubtless kept me from a broken skull. The rock I most resented struck the tip of a horn and made my entire body throb like the clapper of a swinging bell. If they've chipped my horn, I vowed, by Hippos, the god of horses, I will wring their scurvy necks!

Then the door in the trunk opened to disgorge my three workers. I handed Pandia into their multitudinous legs and bounded after them, striking the doorjamb and setting the cowbell to a frantic reverberation. Inside the door, I waved to Icarus and Thea on the walkway below the parapet. Suddenly the pain in my ankle erupted into my head. I was briefly conscious of falling to the ground and, at the same time, falling on sleep. The warm grass seemed a linen coverlet rising to enfold me.

I awoke to Elysium. My head lay in Thea's lap. She was fragrant as always with myrrh and marjoram, and her little hand touched coolness to my forehead. The ghost of a dream lingered in my brain: Before my waking, it seemed, a sweet, incredible fire had touched my lips (a dream surely?). I closed my eyes to recapture the fire.

"I saw you blink, Eunostos. Open your eyes and tell me how you feel."

"First, tell me what happened here."

"When you came with Pandia, those dreadful women had been attacking us for an hour. They are gone now, but they've cut your garden to pieces with their stones."

My grapevines littered the ground like murdered snakes. The parasol hung in tatters, the clay oven had lost its door, and the fig tree looked as if locusts had stripped its branches. It resembled a quarry more than a garden.

I sat up and touched my rock-battered horn; no chips were missing. I stretched my bloodied shoulders; Thea, I found, had eased their smart with a cloth soaked in olive oil. I tested my ankle, which promised to hold my weight.

"We must look for total invasion," I said, and told her about the second army. "First, we shall have to guard against fire. Do you mind a little rain?"

With the help of a stone provided by the Thriae, I narrowed the mouth of my fountain until I had thinned and widened its shower to a misty spray which covered the entire trunk.

"The wood will soak," I explained. "Then it won't be easy to set on fire, even with burning arrows."

Pandia opened her arms to the downfalling spray. "But there isn't a rainbow," she sighed, and entered the house to take a nap. "The better to do battle," she called from the stairs.

Thea, Icarus, and I assumed positions behind the parapet. The workers appeared to be guarding the door. They crouched in six-legged readiness as they momentarily anticipated the assaults of a battering ram.

It was Icarus who sighted the enemy. "Achaeans. Just a few, I think." Probably the main host had gone to attack the Centaurs. "But they have a secret weapon."

The secret weapon advanced gigantically across the clearing, a humped, tented vehicle which somehow moved without wheels. After a few seconds of perplexity, I recognized a harmamaxa, a large wagon invented in Asia Minor and covered with a rounded tent of canvas: Achaean booty, no doubt, from one of their innumerable and far-flung raids. In Babylonia, such vehicles were drawn by horses, but animals are vulnerable to arrows and this harmamaxa was powered by men who, having removed the floor and the wheels, pressed towards us on foot while holding the wagon over their heads and most of their bodies. Thus, except for their feet, which were shod in thick leather boots, they enjoyed complete protection from arrows. Instead of the stationary turtle we had faced this morning, here was a turtle in motion, slow, cumbersome, but almost unassailable from a distance. Through the embrasures in the parapet, we fired a stream of arrows at the rounded roof. They struck in the canvas harmlessly as if they were quills, and the turtle became a porcupine. I looked at Icarus as he fitted an arrow into his bow. His bare chest, sun-bronzed above a green loincloth, rippled with manly muscles. And yet he remained touchingly a boy, pitting his arrows against the well-guarded giants of Ajax. I gazed at Thea in wordless communion. Between us, I tried to say, we will shield him, fight for him, die for him. Somehow, it was always innocent Icarus who seemed to need protecting instead of Thea. Innocence has been called the strongest armor; it is only strong, however, in the company of goddess-fearing Men and godly Beasts; not Achaeans.

"They'll have to come out to attack," said Icarus, wincing at his failure to slow the tortoise. "Then we'll pick them off like the wild pigs they are."

"But they'll be at the wall," I said darkly.

"Eunostos," gasped Thea. "The door has opened. Your workers are leaving the fort!"

Dear Zeus, did they mean to betray us? Perhaps unknowingly I had wounded their pride.

"Bion!" I called, but I heard the frenzied buzz of their battle-cry and knew that they meant to defend us and not betray us. The Achaeans stopped in their tracks. The harmamaxa swayed into rooted stillness.

Attack!

Like angry dogs, they darted between the exposed feet of the Achaeans and slashed at their leather boots with savage pincers. Their hard hides protected them from the half-hearted kicks of Men who were trying to hold a wagon above their heads and most of whom could not see the nature of their attackers. The wagon swayed and lurched as if it were bounding along a rocky road behind a pair of fright-crazed stallions, and finally heaved on its side. Twenty-five terror-stricken Men scrambled to their feet and scurried in all directions to escape the pincers.

Once they were free, however, and face to face with their determined but after all not very sizable attackers, the Achaeans regained their courage. I heard their commander rallying them:

"Strike at their joints, Men!"

Deflecting our arrows with their shields, they struck repeatedly at the waving, root-like limbs, and their sharp-edged swords began to slice through the joints. The result was no less lamentable for being inevitable. My workers were soon hobbling over the grass in complete helplessness, while the warriors struck at the tough but not impervious membrane which joined the halves of their bodies, till the halves lay twitching in separate agony. Thus died my brave and beloved friends, devoted as dogs and far more intelligent; artists of the beautiful as well as warriors.

Icarus was sick at his stomach, and I—well, I ran down the ladder, waving my bow and hurling every oath which came to my tongue: "Butchers!"

"Wolf-lovers!"

"Northerners!" I meant to go to my friends, shieldless though I was, and avenge their dismemberment.

An arrow struck at my feet and jarred me to a halt. "That's what they want," cried Thea, waving her bow. "To lure you into the open and hack you to death. Bar the door and come back to the parapet!" She spoke with the rough urgency of an Amazon, but tears had dampened her tunic and she looked like a little girl who had lost her doll. Rage on behalf of my workers melted to tenderness for the brave girl who, in spite of her grief, had acted to save my life. I barred the door and returned to the parapet to watch the determined Achaeans right their harmamaxa and resume their advance on the fort. Behind them, ten of their comrades had fallen to arrows and Telchin pincers.

Icarus shaded his eyes and pointed to the western sky. Diminutive fly-shapes materialized into nine pairs of Thriae, each pair supporting a branch which in turn supported a large bucket. Directly above the house, they began to tilt the buckets and pour the contents down on our heads. Amber, brown, and yellow in turn, it was much too thick for oil, snaking as it fell like a heavy rope flung at our heads. Honey. It was scalding honey which hissed when it struck the spray from the fountain and, not yet cooled, lashed into streamers and droplets and spattered our skin like a horde of terrible mosquitoes. We slapped at our burns and tried at the same time to raise our bows, but the wavering mist of the fountain distorted our aim, and the Thriae emptied their buckets and wheeled out of range before we could thin their ranks.

By now the harmamaxa had reached the walls and attached itself to the door like a huge fungus. We felt the blows of axes under our sandals. Without leaving their tent, the Achaeans had cut through the canvas wall and now they threatened to smash the oak rectangle of the door. The loss of their comrades had given them room in which to wield their axes.

"Icarus," I said, "help me lift the oven onto the parapet."

His eyes brightened with expectation. "We'll drop it on their heads!"

We dragged, heaved, and wrestled it up the ladder; we poised it, hollow but heavy, above the harmamaxa. "Now!"

The canvas roof, which had stopped a score of arrows, buckled under the oven. A thud. A body-wrenching groan. Hurried movements concealed beneath the partially deflated but still unbroken canvas. Then, again, the deadly crunch of the axe, which hit into wood like a hungry weasel, a little more hungrily with each bit, and would only sate itself when it swung on air.

There were no more ovens to drop on their heads. I considered other defenses. Shower them with arrows when they toppled the door? Charge among them with my battle-axe? The sudden return of the Thriae settled the question.

"Retreat," I shouted. "We can't fight two enemies at the same time."

We scrambled down the ladder, cringing as the hot droplets began to strike our backs, and gained the easeful coolness of the stairs. The last to descend, I paused to stare through the mist of the fountain at the ruined garden and the shredded parasol, the vines and the leafless fig tree. A Beast's love for a garden can be as strong as his love for another Beast, since gardens are beings. Who can say if the poppies dream of butterflies in amethyst clouds, the fig tree dreads the coming of the ravenous bees to puncture its fruit, the vines exult in the sun and, growing warm, drowse in the lengthening shade of a parasol? Dreams, dreads, exultance, and repose—and love, always love. Leaves instead of limbs, but hearts and brains, identity and individuality. It is not necessary to walk in order to love.

The taste of loss was wolf's-bane in my mouth.

At the foot of the stairs, I pulled the lever which loosed a hidden panel and choked the stairwell with earth. The Pharaohs of Egypt utilize the same principle in their tombs to guard their mummies and their boat-shaped catafalques. (Where do you think the Egyptians learned their secret? From my own ancestors.)

"They can dig us out," I said, "but I doubt if they brought any shovels. Achaeans are fighters, not plumbers."

"And if they try?"

"We'll leave by the back door."

"Back door?" cried Thea and Icarus in unison.

"Yes," I said, pausing to heighten their expectation. It is always pleasant to divulge a secret under dramatic circumstances. "You didn't think I would live in a house with a single door, did you? Remember my cave? Two doors, in spite of its apparent rusticity. Here, it's the same. Let me show you."

Between the roots in the far wall of the bedroom, a large stone, the width of my shoulders, rested in gray anonymity. I delivered a sharp blow with my hoof and the stone turned on a pivot to disclose a narrow passageway no taller than a Minotaur on all fours. "It cuts right under the field and comes out in the forest. Tomorrow or the next day, I can slip from the house and reconnoiter to see if the Achaeans have left the trunk. They are not going to stay up there permanently. There are too many riches to steal on other parts of Crete. When I return, I'll rap six times and then you can open the door."

"It's time for supper," said Pandia, rising from her nap in the moss, or rather, rising with the moss and resembling a perambulatory thicket. "Have you beaten off the enemy?"

I told her about our retreat.

"You've laid in supplies, I trust?"

"Adequate but not elaborate."

"We shall just have to diet."

We climbed the ladder to prepare our frugal dinner. In the light of a single lamp, the usually amiable vines looked somber and strangling, as if they might drop on our heads and tighten their leathery tendrils around our necks. Between us lay platters of cheese and the kind of bread called gouros (dough mixed with lentils), a skin of beer, and a cup of water for Pandia. When Pandia asked for sweets, Icarus fetched her a jar of pennyroyal from the workshop. But the sight of the forge and tables without their faithful workers took his appetite.

"Eunostos," he said, "do you think you could say some words in memory of Bion and the others?"

"I'll try," I said, and made up a tiny poem, rough and unpolished but at least loving:

Elegy to a Telchin
Who will guard the nest,
Gather mushrooms now,
Milk his aphid-cow?
Lightly let him rest.

There was a long silence, and then we tried to talk. I touched Thea's hand. "We're perfectly safe down here. They can't reach us without a lot of digging, and we would hear them in time to leave by the back door. Even if they shut off the fountain, dry out the trunk, and set a fire, we're well insulated by the roots."

She forced a smile. "The roots, you say. They look—well, as if they had turned poisonous and begun to watch us."

"Nothing that lives underground will hurt you. Not here, at least. Only the things that come from the surface."

"Achaeans," she said, "and those witchy Thriae. It's all my fault, Eunostos. If I had accepted Ajax's advances, none of this would have happened. He would have taken me back to Mycenae with him as his concubine—Achaeans, they say, are surprisingly gentle to women in their own country—and reared Icarus like his son."

"But you wouldn't have come to the forest. You wouldn't have known about your mother."

"Or you. I don't regret the forest, Eunostos. I regret what I brought with me from the world of Men. I opened a door."

"A forest is like a snake," I said. "Occasionally it needs to shed its skin, just for the sake of change. Sometimes it sheds with the seasons. Now, it is shedding in a different, harsher but still necessary way. It is shedding safety which threatened to become stagnation. You can be sure, though, that its new skin will be strong and beautiful."

"You are being kind," she said, "but not very honest."

Pandia seemed to be napping. She had closed her eyes and opened her mouth. But the rest of us tried to talk and avoid the apprehensions which come with silence.

"I expect," said Icarus, "that the Achaeans want your shop as well as us. The gold, I mean."

"Yes," I said. "To melt down in their own land. You know, they are excellent goldsmiths, if you don't mind morbid subjects. You ought to see their death masks."

"Death masks," said Thea pensively. "And dead vines above our heads. The friendly snakes have died. Or something has killed them."

"Nonsense. It's the way the lamp is burning, it makes us all look dead. Like Pandia there. I think it's time for bed."

Thea and Icarus rose to their feet.

"Take the lamp." I suggested. "I'll light another for myself."

Pandia kept her place.

"Pandia, wake up and come to bed," said Thea. "You'll be more comfortable on the moss." She held the lamp under the girl's face. The round eyes were closed like clenched fist; the vivid mouth was drained to a deathly pallor.

The reason lay at the back of her neck, a small, dark hump. I crushed it between my fingers—its little bones snapped easily; its feathers oozed blood, Pandia's blood—and threw the pulp to the floor with a spasm of uncontrollable shivering. A Strige, a vampire owl. Pandia raised her head and struggled to open her eyes. She rubbed the back of her neck.

"I dreamed of bears. They were chasing me until I was very tired. I couldn't lift my feet. I felt their hot breath on my neck."

I pointed to the crushed body.

She gasped and clung to Icarus. "A Strige?"

"Yes, but we found him in time. You'll feel all right in the morning. It must have flown down the stairs while we were fighting the Thriae in the garden. No doubt, they sent it to devil us. Rats, moths, all night-flying creatures are their friends. There may be others."

We searched the house, sifting the moss on the floor of the bedroom, peering under the tables in the workshop, standing on benches with a raised lamp to examine the roof of the den, and found a second Strige, balled among the roots and apparently asleep. Soft, brown, seemingly all feather, he looks as harmless as a baby rabbit, but I knew that he lived on blood, which he sucked so unobtrusively that the victim might die without discovering his presence. If you find an animal dead in the forest for no apparent reason, examine the back of his neck for the marks of two small fangs.

Thea was visibly shaken. She put a protective arm around Pandia's shoulder and whispered, "My dear, it's all right now. This will never happen to you again."

"Yes," I said, "it's all right, but I think we shall all feel safer sleeping together in the bedroom."

We lay close to each other, Icarus, Thea, Pandia, and I, shared the warmth of hope in one of those bleak and endless-seeming hours which end as surely as banqueting, games and love. Pandia clutched my hand until she fell asleep, and then I held her fingers, her almost-paw, loving her tenderly (yet wishing, must I confess, that she was Thea). I was tired and sad and missing my workers, and my wounded ankle throbbed as if the tentacles of an octopus alternately squeezed and released, squeezed and released the parted flesh. The usually soft moss aggravated the bruises and burns on my back.

I awoke in the night, when the thinly flickering flame announced the near-exhaustion of its oil. Thea was gone. I thought: she has gone to give herself to the Achaeans.

Chapter X

WOLF'S-BANE

"I'm going to get her back," I said when Icarus and Pandia, awakened by urgent shakes, blinked in the light of the dying lamp. "I'm going to get her back, and kill that murderous Ajax. He's a wicked Man, and his Men are wolves, and they will not leave this forest with Thea." I felt like the stony bed of a stream in summer, dry and parched and sprayed with the fine dust which blows from Libya. I felt—untenanted.

"I'm going too," said Icarus.

I shook my head and explained impatiently why he and Pandia ought to stay in the house, she for protection, he to protect her.

"I can go where you can't," he continued, the rare soldier who knows the rare time when he ought to question his commander. "They can see your red hair for a mile, and even when you stoop, you look as big as a griffin. But I can sneak. I'm very good at it. At Vathypetro, I learned to sneak out of the palace when I was six years old, and I've been practicing ever since."

"I'm going too," said Pandia. "I can't sneak but I can bite." She bared her small but numerous teeth. "They're made for fish heads as well as berries."

"Someone has to stay here," I explained to her. "To let Icarus and me back in the house. You'll be quite safe. If you hear any tunneling, then and only then you can leave by the back door."

Pandia acquiesced with such ill humor that I hesitated to turn my back and risk my tail within the range of her teeth. Fortunately, Icarus mollified her with a brotherly kiss on her head. Girded with loincloths and armed with daggers, we bent to enter the tunnel. In a limited space, we did not wish to be encumbered with bows and arrows.

The tunnel was never tall enough in which to stand, and only sometimes tall enough in which to crawl; sometimes we had to wriggle on our stomachs, scraping our bare legs and chests over roots and stones, and I found myself forcibly reminded that my workers had built the passage for their own peregrinations and not for the egress of a seven-foot Minotaur and the five-foot son of a Dryad.

"Icarus," I called behind me, booming in the cramped, earthen corridor like the angry Bull-God before he sends an earthquake. "We are going to come to some water which leads out of the tunnel. I'll go first. If everything is clear outside, I'll swim back and get you. Otherwise, wait a few minutes and then return to the house."

The underground water was almost as cold as the melting snow which fed it in the mountains. I dived, negotiated a passage the size of a door, and slid to the surface in the same stream which ran by Pandia's village. I sent the merest of ripples widening to the bank, where a large water rat eyed me from the mouth of a burrow belonging to a Paniscus, and green branches swayed in the current like the trees of drowned Dryads. I returned for Icarus and, shivering violently, both of us climbed onto the bank and shook ourselves to restore warmth.

"Eunostos," he chattered. "R-remember when you s-said that one day we would be old c-comrades facing battle together?"

"Yes."

"Well," he said. "We are. Not old, but comrades. I want you to know that wherever you are, I am. To fight at your side and stand guard when you fall asleep. I want you to know that you are—friended."

I have known two loves, I thought, one for a girl who wished to be my sister and therefore cut me like broken coral; one for a boy who wished to be my brother and therefore comforted me like the moss in which I sleep. If I had died before they came to the forest, my soul would have been a serpent, kind but ugly and earthbound. Now it will be a butterfly, and no barriers of wind will hold me from the perilous chasms of the clouds or the tawny orchards of the sunflower.

Warmed at last, we crept to the edge of the field which held my house. A tendril of smoke arose from the garden, like a beansprout climbing the sky, and the scent of venison piqued our nostrils.

"The swine," said Icarus. "Gorging themselves in your house."

"Yes," I said, "but at least they haven't burned it."

"Think of the housecleaning after they're gone," he sighed. "Bones in the fountain. Grape skins on the bench. And you know"—he lowered his voice—"they won't bother to use the watercloset."

When we turned from the house to pursue our mission, the snake Perdix coiled at our feet.

"Uncle," said Icarus, muffling his joyful cry into a whisper. He clasped the snake in his hand and addressed him with great solemnity, careful to speak each word with separate emphasis. "Did you know that Thea has been captured?"

Perdix opened his mouth and flickered his forked tongue.

"He understands," explained Icarus. "It's the only way he can communicate, since I've never learned to speak in real snake. He really does understand what I say. Not everything, of course. Adjectives give him trouble. But if I speak slowly, he catches the nouns and verbs. That time when Ajax was chasing Thea, just before we came to the forest, it was I who sent Perdix into the room to make Ajax angry. He can help us now, I think." He restored Perdix to his familiar haunt in the pouch of his loincloth. I was still not convinced that the snake could help our mission, but I dared not belittle him within the range of his fangs.

Icarus with his snake was no longer a child with a pet. Rather, he treated Perdix as a warrior treats a dependable ally, a horse or a war dog, with trust, affection, and dignity. The three of us headed toward the town of the Centaurs, the obvious place for the main host of Achaeans and also for Thea's surrender.

Along the way, we found that Ajax had preceded us to Pandia's village. No house had escaped a pilfering, and Pandia's log had been split down the middle by an axe. Shattered crockery and a few smoked fish, evidently not to the taste of the conquerors, testified to what had once been her well-stocked larder. They had emptied her Cretan Bears-tail out of its pot, as if they suspected a cache of coins, and worst of all, they had turned the communal berry patch into a small wilderness of raucous crows, uprooted posts, and stripped vines. The Bears themselves, it appeared, had been captured by Ajax and carried on his march.

Icarus glanced at the crows and scattered them with a well-aimed handle from a honey pot. "I'm glad Pandia didn't come," he said. "It would have broken her heart."

"Or turned her stomach," I said, and resumed our journey with revenge as well as rescue to spur my hooves.

We approached the farms of the Centaurs with great stealth, in case the besieging Ajax had stationed guards to protect his rear. Where the forest met the vineyards, Icarus climbed a tree to locate the enemy. I myself am not adept at climbing (except the oaks of Dryads). The branches have a way of buckling under my weight or catching my tail. But Icarus insinuated himself into the foliage with a skill which did credit to his mother's race; and after his reconnoitering, extricated himself without a rustle.

A cobweb stretched over one of his eyes and gave him the look of a pirate, and a pirate's ferocity crackled in his voice when he told me what he had seen.

"They are not besieging," he said. "They have already captured the town! It's too far to see clearly, but I could just make out bands of helmeted men wandering through the streets, as if they owned the place. I'll have to move closer to get a real look."

"Wait till night. Then we'll go together."

Darkness is a going instead of a coming; absence of light rather than a presence of bat wings, mummy wrappings, ravens, or whatever other fanciful figure of speech we poets use to describe her. But a going can be as welcome as a coming, and daylight, hateful for what it showed, faded like a lamp which has burned its olive oil and left us to the kind secrecy of night. We crossed the vineyards, their green grapelets invisible beneath a moonless sky, and bypassed the compound to avoid exciting the animals. We saw, after first hearing, two Achaean patrols. They had been celebrating; they were still imbibing. They sang or laughed as they made their rounds, and paused whenever they met to swap convivialities. Under their belts they carried little flasks which they swapped and tipped to their mouths with a maximum of contented smacks. It was not hard to avoid them. If they saw us at all, they must have mistaken us for a pair of palm trees with broad trunks and without fronds.

We came to the clump of olive trees which I had previously noticed beside the moat, and one of them looked so staunch and concealing that I felt emboldened to risk my weight in the branches. I saw that most of the Achaeans had gathered in the theater to hold a banquet. They had built a fire in the pit and, using their swords as spits, begun to roast their dinner. Thea, our precious, surrendered Thea, sat on one of the tiers and seemed oblivious to men, fire, and food. The earless Xanthus pointed toward the fire as if to say: "Will you share in our feast?" She shook her head. "Thea," I wanted to cry, "accept his invitation. Your supper last night was a bit of cheese and a slice of bread. You went to the Achaeans of your own will and now you must eat their food in order to keep your strength." Then I discovered the reason for her abstinence. The Men were eating not only the domesticated pigs of the Centaurs, but some of the blue monkeys from the forest. The skinned and spitted bodies were clearly recognizable in the light of the fire, as eager cooks jostled each other to lower them into the flames and turn them from side to side. Blue monkeys. Thea's monkeys. The forest's laughter, she had said. I thought of what she must feel to have them offered her on a spit or a platter.

The men who were not cooking tippled from horns or wineskins, sang ribald songs about the women of their conquests—raw-boned Israelites who would slip a knife in your back when you closed your eyes; olive-skinned Egyptians who bragged about their sphinxes and pyramids and made you feel like crass barbarians; and Cretans with bare breasts who were good mistresses once they had satisfied their pride by making a show of resistance. One man sang a ballad about the famous Cretan bosom, which he variously compared to anthills, burial mounds, and helmets, none of them happy comparisons, it seemed to me (being a poet, perhaps I am too critical). Laughter, coarse and brutal, interrupted the songs, and Ajax, the swaggering victor, moved among his Men, drank their wine, and claimed the tenderest morsels from their swords.

Thus, the conquerors. The conquered lay in the streets. The sad, ungainly bodies of those gracious farm-folk, the Centaurs, together with splintered houses, broken lanterns, and torn tapestries, attested to a fierce battle in the very heart of the town. The surviving Centaurs, I saw, had been shut in the animal compound with their sheep and oxen and were now being guarded by a small contingent of soldiers, most of whom stood at the gate while two of their number patrolled the high and virtually unclimbable walls of thorn. None of the males had survived the battle; and a handful of females and children, along with the hapless Bears of Artemis and three Panisci, comprised the prisoners. I felt as I had when I saw my workers slaughtered before my eyes; if anything, worse, for Centaurs are higher beings, no less loyal and far more kind and intelligent. Chiron, the blameless king. Moschus, a bore but lovable: their faces came to haunt me, noble of mane, and the thunder of their hooves. But tears are a luxury not permitted to warriors on the threshold of battle. I stifled my grief into a far corner of my brain and let my anger flare like the fires in the forge of Hephaestus, the smithy god, when he works his bellows: anger which spurs the body to valor, the mind to craft.

"Those poor Centaurs," said Icarus when we had left our trees and met to whisper plans. "And the blue monkeys. How do you think the Achaeans got them?" It was the lingering child in him which lamented the Centaurs and the monkeys with the same grief.

"They are trusting creatures. Ajax may have lured them right into the town with the offers of food. Or maybe they followed Thea."

"I wish we could enter the town as easily as the monkeys."

I deliberated. "Perhaps we can send a weapon even if we can't go ourselves."

"A secret weapon?" The harmamaxa had fascinated him. But the weapon I had in mind was less obvious and much more devilish.

"Remember my telling you about our war with the wolves and how Chiron thought of feeding them wolf's-bane? It's a rather innocuous looking root, a bit like a dark carrot. But the monkeys love roots of all kinds. If we could get them to eat wolf's-bane, and drive them toward the town before they died—"

"The Achaeans would eat them, but Thea wouldn't. They would poison themselves!"

"Exactly."

"Is the poison always fatal?"

"When taken in sufficient quantities. Smaller quantities act like a sedative. Either way, the enemy would be knocked out long enough for us to release the captives and take the town."

We spent the night in my cave, sitting back to back and sharing each other's warmth in the damp, cold air: friend and friend, remembering what we had lost; warrior and warrior, plotting tomorrow's vengeance and what we hoped to win.

Icarus said at last: "Eunostos, I am cold all over except for my back," and I cradled him in my arms until he slept. He had no wish to remain a child, but it pleased him for the moment to relax from the stance of a warrior into the old childish ways of need and dependence, and it pleased his friend to father and shield him.

It is one of the ways of love to delight in the youngness, the littleness, the helplessness of the beloved.

When the sun crept yellow feelers into the cave, we went to look for wolf's-bane. The plant had never thrived on temperate Crete. Its favorite habitat is the cold northern mountains of the mainland, where the sun is a sometime visitor instead of a king.

"Perdix will help us," Icarus announced. "A snake should know about the roots of all kinds. He lives among them." He drew the snake from his pouch and addressed him with tenderness. "Don't you, Perdix?"

"Does he understand the word 'wolf's-bane?'"

"It explains itself, doesn't it?" To the snake he said with great emphasis: "WOLF'S-BANE. ROOTS TO KILL A WOLF."

The tongue flickered with what I presumed to be comprehension and perhaps a touch of petulance because Icarus spoke to him as if he had no tongue to catch the vibrations of human speech. Icarus stooped to release him and, before he could touch the ground, the snake escaped from his fingers. We hurried to follow him through the undergrowth.

"I think he's after a female," I whispered when the sweat of the chase had begun to mat my hair.

"He's doing his bit for Thea. After all, she's his great-great-niece. Though," he admitted, "I expect he loves me best. I've never stepped on his tail."

Possessed of a tail myself (though its altitude preserves it from treading sandals), I could understand the snake's preference.

In less than an hour, he led us to the ragged and unscalable cliff which formed the eastern boundary of the forest. In the shadow of the cliff and the further shade of a large carob tree, we found a clump of wolf's-bane. Like their four-legged namesake, the plants prefer shadows to sunlight. I knew that in late summer they would burst into showy but somewhat sinister hooded flowers, like visored helmets, of blue, yellow, purple, or white; now, however, leaves like slender, tapering hands. We pulled them up by their stalks and shook the dirt from their thick, tuberous roots. They did not look appetizing, but neither does a carrot, a raw fish, or a plucked chicken.

It was not hard to find a congregation of blue monkeys, the happiest of animals and perhaps the most talkative. You can hear that chattering from a great distance, a multitude of cries which merge their separate sharpnesses into a single music. Merry, trusting, affectionate, they recognized Icarus and me as familiar faces and, at the same time, spied the bait in our hands. One of them jumped on my shoulders and, twining his legs around my neck, bent to clutch at a root. I made a soft chattering which I supposed to approximate monkey and gestured toward the town of the Centaurs, as if to say that I would feed him when we reached the town.

I looked at Icarus and saw the tears in his eyes. "We're killing them for Thea," I reminded him. "To save her from those ruffians."

"I know," he said, "but treachery is still treacherous. Otherwise, why are you crying?"

"I'm not crying," I snapped so sharply that the monkey jumped from my shoulder. "I'm trying to comfort you."

"You're always trying to comfort someone—Thea, Pandia, me—and doing very well at it. In fact, you're the most comfortable person I know. But sometimes you need comforting too. I think you ought to marry Thea as soon as you rescue her."

He did not doubt that we would be successful or that, once rescued, she would wish to marry me. To be admired by such a boy—well, it made me want to reach and aspire until my heart more nearly equaled my height.

The monkeys followed us in a long, vociferous stream, and I earnestly hoped that no Achaeans would issue from the trees to contest our advance. Once, a Dryad called to us from her bower, her face poised in the branches like a water lily in a green pool. In the past she had always scorned me, but now she called in a husky whisper:

"Eunostos, take care of yourself. The forest depends on you."

At the edge of the forest, still under cover of trees, we fed the monkeys. With a touching but not entirely successful attempt to avoid biting or scratching us, they plucked the roots from our hands and ate them so quickly that they did not have time to notice their bitterness. Then we waved our daggers and ran at the unsuspecting creatures with a show of great ferocity. At first they mistook our actions for a game and tried to wrestle the knives out of our hands. We had to strike them with the flats of our blades to prove our hostility. I shall never forget their cries of astonishment and disbelief. We watched them vaulting across the trellises of the vineyard, still in a pack and more aggrieved than frightened.

We could not follow them into the fields by daylight, but Icarus, climbing another tree, witnessed the meeting between the monkeys and the Achaeans, who heard their arrival and came from the compound to investigate. Already the monkeys were growing sluggish with the poison, which strikes painlessly but with first a tingling and then a deadening of all sensations, and the men dispatched them with swords and returned to the compound. The Achaeans, who were not acquainted with monkey's usual vigor, had no reason to suspect their condition. They received the congratulations of their

friends on a good catch; they paused; they seemed to deliberate, no doubt asking themselves if they ought to share their
prize with those in the town. Generosity or fear of Ajax provided the answer, and selecting the plumpest to keep in the
compound, they strung the remaining bodies on a rope and
headed for the town.

When the absence which is night had made our presence reasonably undiscoverable, we crossed the fields and,
encountering no patrols, resumed our vantage points in the
trees beside the moat. Two bonfires writhed in darkness, like
orange squids in the lightless depths of the sea: one in the
theater, one in the compound. It was the many-tentacled fire
in the theater which held my attention.

Tonight the Achaeans did not lack women. They seemed
to have spent the afternoon hunting in the woods, and three
Dryads, drawn and haggard, their long hair disheveled and,
in places, apparently torn out by the roots, represented their
catch. I rejoiced that Zoe was not among them. The four
queens of the Thriae and several of the drones had also come
to the banquet, but as guests instead of captives and of course
without the workers, who are not endowed for orgies. The four
queens strutted around the pit as if they had conquered the
forest through their own prowess, and they jangled more than
their usual number of bracelets—spoils, no doubt, from the
gutted homes of the Centaurs. Later, I learned that the queens
had indeed proved helpful traitors by surprising the Centaurs
in the gate-tower and lowering the bridge to Ajax's Men. The
hope occurred to me that they might forget themselves in the
flush of victory and scatter their fatal kisses among their allies, but they chose to stand on their dignity as queens—they
smiled and received compliments but did not descend to the
familiarities of love. The drones, however, simpered like
courtesans among the rugged Achaeans, who, along with the
Cretans, enjoy a considerable versatility in sexual practices,
and Amber's brother seemed to be collecting a small fortune
in arm-bands, pendants, and rings.

Achaeans are altogether indiscriminate in their pleasures. They can eat, drink, and wench in the same breath, and tonight they lost no time in cooking the blue monkeys, together with fish, venison, and the last of the Centaur's pigs. Even while fondling a skin of wine, a drone, or a Dryad, they lifted the deadly meat to their lips and ate with relish. Haunches and limbs were passed from hand to hand until everyone received at least a modicum of the tender meat and enough poison, I trusted, to drug even if not to kill him. On the topmost row of the theater, a sly little chap concealed himself in the shadows to enjoy an undivided monkey, but three of his comrades followed him from the pit, dismembered the animal, and left him only the head, which however, he ate without protest. The vegetarian Thriae did not partake of the meat, nor did the Dryads, and when Ajax presented a skinny leg to Thea, she flung it in his face. He slapped her onto the stones, retrieved the leg, and shredded the meat from the bone with one raking bite.

"Bloody barbarian," I muttered. "I'll ram that bone right down your throat."

"Shhhhhh," warned Icarus. "You're starting to bellow. After we rescue Thea, you can ram it anywhere you like."

When men have drunk enough wine to float a penteconter and eaten enough meat to sink a round-built merchant ship, they usually want to sleep, but the sudden sleep which overpowered the Achaeans resembled the miasmic mists which rise from the bowels of Sicily and prostrate travelers when they leave their litters to drink at wayside fountains. They began to slump on the stairs; they stretched in the pit, swords clattering, wine cups falling from limp fingers. Those who had eaten lightly succumbed more slowly; had time in which to view their friends with dazed astonishment before they joined them in heaped and sprawling confusion.

The Thriae could not account for the strange sleep of their hosts. Intoxicated? Drugged? Exhausted by the rigors of conquest? They fluttered above the prostrated bodies, their dulcet tones growing shrill; they shouted, prodded with jeweled fingers, clamored—the queens for attention, the drones for caresses. Quietly the three Dryads congregated around Thea and began to help her collect the Achaean daggers.

Amber, kneeling to prod a recumbent body, lifted her head to confront an armed and determined Thea, who seized the gauzy membrane of her wing and delivered a slap which spun her head as if it had been struck by the boom of a sail. By now the drones and the other queens had mounted the air, and the oldest queen, she of the mottled skin and bulging eyes, pelted Thea with bracelets until the girl relaxed her hold on Amber's wing. With a fury of fluttering, Amber rejoined her sisters and called to Thea as if she were spitting:

"Dearest one, I hope that a Strige will suck your blood and blue-flies pick your bones."

The Thriae began to mass above the pit, stripping their bracelets to use as missiles; though one of the queens was old, and the drones were effeminate cowards, Thea and three harassed Dryads could hardly hope to repel an attack.

"Thriae," I boomed, "I am coming to get you with my army!" I thrashed about in my tree like a small whirlwind, and my army of one gave a roar which suggested Minotaur in his veins.

The Thriae retreated with such precipitous haste that two of the drones collided and almost fell to the ground before they could disentangle their wings and, casting regretful looks at the prone, manly bodies of their allies, flutter after their queens. It is said that queens, drones, and workers flew to the land of the Achaeans to live on Mount Parnassus, deliver oracles of doubtful authority, and receive the tribute accorded to deities. (If this were a tale instead of a history, you may rest assured that I would have drowned them in the sea like Icarus' namesake, the ill-fated son of Daedalus.)

Thea and the Dryads resumed their task of disarming the Achaeans. Some were dead or dying; some would awaken with wracking pains and without weapons. Ajax, kneeling dazedly beside his friend Xanthus, struggled to his feet and held his great sword between him and the girl who had caused his ruin.

"She-wolf," he groaned. "I am going to kill you." For a wicked man attributes his own sins, his own wolfishness, to those who oppose him.

Slowly, laboriously, he raised the sword above his head, as if through fathoms of water. She did not wait for its descent; she drove her dagger between his ribs. The sword fell from his hand and clattered onto the stones. At first, he did not fall, but faced her with draining defiance.

"Goddess," he said, and crumpled at her feet, his yellow beard pressing against her sandals.

She stared at his body with stricken horror. Even from a distance, I saw the rigidity of her arms and the enormity of her eyes. But she did not weep. She had killed a man and the act appalled her, but the gods had forced her hand. She knelt to remove his dagger.

Icarus and I climbed from our tree. First we entered the compound and, disarming the drugged or slain Achaeans, released the prisoners. No one spoke; there are no appropriate words to greet a victory which comes too late and at too great a cost.

Finally, I said: "We will go to the town and bring the survivors to the compound where we can watch them."

They trooped after me in a proud and sorrowful file.

The Panisci, furtive and mysterious, vanished into the night to return to their burrows in the banks of the stream. I thought: I will feed the Bears of Artemis from the leavings of the Achaean feast—the fish and the venison—and make them beds under the stars with the fatherless children of the Centaurs.

"Thea," I called across the moat. "Will you lower the bridge for us?"

She came to me along the path which Chiron had walked in the time before the invasion, a woman who, at sixteen, had put behind her the girlhood which, even at Vathypetro, had been shadowed by the owl-wings of maturity. The Dryads followed her in deference and awe. At last she was one of them, utterly, yet also the strongest of them.

"Thea," I said, as she walked from the glowing heart of the fire, out of the light and into the darkness; salamander, phoenix, goddess, illuminating the great fastnesses of the night and my own heart.

Chapter XI

THE PASSING OF THE BEASTS

Twenty-one Achaeans in all had survived the poison. Those in the theater stirred with fitful groans and rolled their heads as if to dislodge the demons that haunted their dreams. We lost no time in carrying them to join their comrades in the compound.

"After I surrendered, they refused to leave the forest," Thea explained when the drowsy warriors, clutching their stomachs or rubbing their eyes, were safely lodged behind the walls of thorn. "According to Ajax, I had caused him so much trouble that he meant to repay himself with all the riches in the forest. If I showed him the underground passage to your workshop, he promised to set me free. Of course I showed him nothing."

"What did he intend to do with you? Take you back to Mycenae?"

"I think he intended to kill me. Somehow, I seemed to frighten him. He called me the Beast Princess."

"He was right, you know."

* * * *

The next morning, while Icarus entered my house through the tunnel to rescue Pandia, I led a band of Panisci to the edge of the field and blared a challenge to the garrison in the trunk. The Panisci were armed with slings, I with a battle-axe, and we dragged a red-eyed Xanthus on a rope to corroborate our claims to victory. The Achaeans were not long in appearing behind the parapet. I could see the glint of their helmets through the embrasures.

"We have won the war," I boomed, "and killed your leader, Ajax. Those of your friends who survive are now our hostages. If you wish to save them and yourselves, discard your weapons and leave the forest before sunset."

They greeted my claims with derisive laughter. Smug in their captured retreat, feasting from cockcrow to the time of lamps, they had good reason to scorn the ultimatum.

We jerked our captive out of the trees and flaunted him in his ignominious ruin.

"Listen to them," he urged his friends. "Ajax is truly dead and every one of us has been poisoned by their magic." He pressed his stomach for emphasis. "It will get you too unless you do as he says!"

Laughter yielded to consultation, excited voices to the groan of the crude timbers which served as a door. Framed in the doorway behind his shield, a single warrior addressed us. His insolence could not conceal his fear:

"Send us Xanthus and let us question him."

We could spare one hostage to prove our claims. An eager Paniscus prodded him with his sling, and the earless Xanthus, dragging his rope and casting timorous glances over his shoulder, reeled to join his friends.

Led by Xanthus, the Achaeans left my house in the afternoon, and the next morning we sent their comrades from the compound to overtake and join them beyond the forest. I had taken their weapons, armor, and tunics and, knowing the Achaeans cultivate their beards as the visible sign of valor, I had forced them to shave with a coarse bronze razor which left their cheeks the color of a radish. Kings and conquerors, they had come to humble us, and they left like a column of slaves being marched to the infamous marketplace in Pylos.

Again, the forest belonged to the Beasts, but to people whose heroes are dead, whose towns lie in ruins, and who must momentarily expect another invasion, the taste of victory can be as bitter as hemlock.

Two weeks after the departure of the Achaeans, a patrol of Panisci caught a Cretan just as he entered the forest and brought him none too gently to the town of the Centaurs, where Thea, Icarus, and I were helping the females to rebuild their houses. Black-haired, narrow-waisted, thin as the peasants who live in the reed hovels along the Nile, he blinked nervously; he looked like a man who had come from a long and grueling battle, not yet won. Aeacus, of course, had sent him.

"Thea," I called, wanting secretly to butt him into the moat. "Will you bring your guest some coconut milk?" It was all we had to offer. The Achaeans had drunk our wine, and the grapes were not yet ripe. I left him with Thea and Icarus in one of the bamboo stalls, newly rebuilt and hung with the few silks which had not been dirtied by the boots of the conquerors or used to clean their armor.

I crossed the bridge. Every evening, usually with Thea and Icarus, I returned to my house to work and sleep. Centaur females patrolled the moat and guarded the animals—two cows, a bull, seven sheep—which remained in the compound.

"They have come for your friends?" asked the Centaur whose name was Rhode, daughter of the noble Chiron. Before the war, she had worn a white lily in her hair. She had cut her hair the day of her father's death, and the short tresses no longer could hold a stem.

"Yes, Rhode."

"Will Thea and Icarus return with the Cretan?"

"I don't know."

"There will always be someone who comes to invade our peace. They will never leave us alone, will they, Eunostos? Isn't it time we left the forest? Returned to the Isles?"

The Isles of the Blest, she meant. The land in the Western Sea from which we had come, in the age before men: a pleasant and sunny land, without dangers—and also without adventures.

"The gods will tell us the time," I said. "It will be soon, I think."

I waited in my garden for Thea and Icarus. In the ivory moonlight, the fountain swayed like a rain-drenched palm touching the earth with its fronds. I had dug a new staircase under the ground, and of course my workshop and other rooms had escaped the depredations of war. Not the garden, however. There was no parasol, and my fig tree had been uprooted and burned for wood. My trellises were bare, and the new seeds I had planted had not had time to sprout. It was still a garden without greenery.

"Knossos has not yet fallen," said Thea excitedly when she arrived with Icarus. "Our father is still fighting. He learned from Xanthus, who is now his captive, that Icarus and I were here in the forest. He could not come himself because the city is under siege. But he sent his messenger to urge us to stay where we are until the war is won. That's what my father says, but—"

"But you want to go to him. You think you can help him."

The ardor died from her voice. "I don't want to go," she said dully. "I want to stay here with you and our friends. But he is my father, and the Cretans were once my people. In spite of their faults, they are better than Achaeans. It will be bad for all of us if Knossos falls."

"And what can you and Icarus do to keep it from falling?"

"You yourself have taught us how to fight."

Silence returned to the garden; silence, except for the cricket-voices of the fountain and the quick breaths of Icarus, who looked at me with the unquestioning worship of a boy who expected the one decisive action, the one infallible command which would solve his dilemma.

"I don't want to go back to my father," he said. "He was like a shadow. He carried darkness wherever he walked."

"Sadness," said Thea. "Not darkness."

"Whatever it was, it was cold. You couldn't touch him, you know. He had a way of drawing back as if your fingers might dirty his robe. It's you I love, Eunostos. Haven't I become a Beast?"

"You always were," said Thea. "You didn't have to come here, as I didn't to find the Beast in you. Perhaps you ought to go back to find the Man. At least, a little of him."

"What Thea means," I said, "is that you and I, Icarus, have hearts like forests. Maybe we need to cut down a few of the trees and build a city."

"Or save a city," she said. "Knossos. Will you come with me, Icarus? If only for a little?"

For a little? Forever, I thought.

"Must I go, Eunostos?"

"Thea will need you," I said, wrenching the words like an arrow from my heart. I held him in my arms for the last time. I held the young forest before it had lost the singing of its sweetest birds and the lifting of its tallest trees; I held its fawn and rabbit, bear cub and pink Paniscus with cloven hooves and tail like the curl of a grapevine, and the warm fledgling of the woodpecker, enclosed in his fort of twigs; all things small, vulnerable, and hopeful, all things that wish to grow. But I could not arrest the passage of that treacherous lizard, time.

"Icarus," I said. It was neither a cry nor a plea, but the simple, final utterance of a name which I loved. I did not watch him when he left the garden.

We sat in the midst of the fountain as if it could wash our pain to the insubstantiality of moonlight. The sadness of moonlight is real but a little remote. Stars cry out in loneliness, and the moon, I think, is the loneliest of goddesses. Still, they are far away, and the loss they tell has the wistful sweetness of a tale about the maidenhood of the Great Mother or an old song sung by the Dryads when they turn their handmills and grind the barley to flour. But the sadness of a house and a garden is different and very close; as close as the hot coal which burns your hand or the captured bat which screams to free itself from the tangle of your hair.

"I had hoped," she said, "to see your trellises hold new vines." She caught my hand between the coldness of her fingers. "Eunostos, it is a Man's—or a Beast's—tragedy that two loves may call him in different directions. By following one, he is bound to leave the other. Leave, I say, not lose. No love is ever lost. It changes its form like water, from lake to river to cloud, and when we are most a desert, it falls from the sky in fructifying rain."

"I don't know about rain," I said. "I was never a philosopher, and I'm no longer a poet. If you have to go, I want to go with you. Protect you till you join your father and then fight in his army. You know I can fight. You've seen me with my bow!"

"How can you leave your people? There is only you to lead them. You see, my dear, you also have two loves. Those with a single love—how poor they are! Ajax and war, and Thriae and gold. Ours is the treasure of pharaohs."

"I don't feel like a pharaoh. I fell like a palm tree without any coconuts."

"You'll get them back. And blue monkeys to play in your branches. I'm going to leave you now. You must close your eyes. They stare and stare and ask what I cannot give."

Her sandals leaving the garden were as hushed as the hooves of a fawn.

* * * *

Aeacus did not forget the Beasts who had sheltered his children. He sent a second messenger, who drank from a coconut in the house of a Centaur, loosened the belt which constricted his narrow waist, and told me about the war. The Achaean army, it seemed, had fought to the gates of the palace, which, lacking the walls of mainland citadels like Mycenae and Tiryns, had been frantically buttressed with timbers, rubble, and even the stone bathtubs from the royal suite. Aeacus himself lay wounded and close to death when its battered Cretans, among them Icarus, marched through the corbelled arch of the gate to what appeared to be their last and mortal defeat. But even while the lamentation of the women resounded through the gardens and the pillared courtyards, the Princess

Thea appeared on the walls and urged her warriors to victory in the name of the Great Mother and the Minotaur. The besieging Achaeans gasped when they saw her beauty: the crimson, helmet-shaped skirt emblazoned with jet-black ants; the bared breasts, flaunting fertility in the very graveyard of war; the golden serpents coiled around her wrist; the pointed ears; the greenly tumbled hair which lent to her chiseled features a wild and intoxicating barbarism.

Archers forgot to draw their bows. Swordsmen fell to their knees and raised their swords like talismans above their heads.

A hush and then an outcry.

"Sorceress!"

"Goddess!"

"Beast Princess!"

It was then that the boy Icarus charged them with his shield Bion. They saw his pointed ears. They knew him to be her brother. They had come to fight puny Men—sailors and merchants and perfumed courtiers—and not these bright, avenging children from the Country of the Beasts.

"The Beast Prince!"

They stared; they dropped their weapons. They reeled toward the sea, trampling vineyards, stampeding goats among the hillocks of red poppies, fleeing the Children of the Beasts. To their wooden ships they fled, scrambling up the hulls like avid crabs, hoisting the black sails until they bellied with wind and bore them away and away from the sword-strewn beach and the boy who waved his shield and hurled after them the curse of the Minotaur.

"And now," concluded the messenger, flushed with the telling, "the smoke of hecatombs has made a forest of the afternoon. Burnt offerings to the god of battles! Sandarac and myrrh in the caves of the Great Mother! Flowers gathered from the liberated fields—poppies and roses, violets and asphodels to garland the victors. Thea, the Beautiful, and Icarus, Prince of Warriors. Aeacus himself was carried to watch the garlanding. He has not forgotten your kindness to his children nor the loss you suffered fighting against Achaeans. It is he who has sent me to offer you the gift of two ships to return you to the safety of your homeland, the Isles of the Blest. His own sailors will man them, and no country is beyond their sailing. You will find both ships at the port of Phaestus. They will be provisioned on your arrival."

* * * *

I carried with me only the wicker basket from my picnic with Thea and Icarus, and in it my green tunic, a flask of beer, a few honey cakes, a reed pen, and some strips of papyrus (you see, I had started to write my history); and over my shoulder a hoe. There would always be gardens.

I met my friends in the town of the Centaurs. Pandia led the Bears, who had never returned to live in their own village with its plundered logs and withered vines. In spite of her tender years, she had won a name for being something of an Amazon and she bared her teeth proudly as the Girls trooped after her across the drawbridge, the oldest of them looking no more than twelve and holding the hands of daughters or granddaughters who might have been their sisters.

"Wouldn't Icarus be proud to see me?" she said.

"Yes," I said, "and so am I."

Next came the Centaur children, some of them very young and trying to gallop in several directions at once, and last, the mothers with their few belongings strapped to their backs: a lantern, a wicker cage for crickets (empty), a coverlet for cold nights at sea. At the edge of the woods, we found the Dryads waiting in covered litters built from their trees. After they had boarded the ships, the wooden hulls would protect them until they could find new trees in the Isles of the Blest. The Panisci had offered to carry them. You would have hardly recognized the once mischievous goat boys as they lifted the litters on their hairy shoulders and moved through the forest with no attempt to frighten their passengers or race their friends. I took my place at the head of the company.

"Eunostos," called Zoe from her litter. "Will you walk beside me?"

She had started to look her three hundred and seventy years. Was this the great-hearted temptress who had danced the Dance of the Python and emptied a skin of beer with a few gulps? No longer did she stir my blood, but she stirred my heart to a deep, aching tenderness.

She took my hand. "You're not the Eunostos I used to love. You have—how shall I say?—grown up."

"Up, perhaps. Not wise."

"A truly wise man is too modest to recognize his own wisdom. If I had not grown old while you were growing up, I could have loved you the best of all my lovers!"

The trees of the Dryads, denuded of branches to build the litters, had dropped their leaves in premature autumn. The village of the Bear Girls had been entirely occupied by the crows, who had gutted the logs and the berry patch with the thoroughness of a forest fire, and the burrows of Panisci had fallen to water rats who, with twigs and mud, were busy diminishing the large entrances to their own size. Do you know the story that the Forest was once a god, young as the sun who steps from the sea in the morning? That he ruled the earth until the Coming of the Great Mother and then willingly retired to the foot of the hills with memories enough to content him for many centuries? If the story is true, I think he has now grown tired of remembering.

* * * *

Our ships ride at anchor, sturdy of cypress, twin-masted, with dolphin-shaped pennants hanging from the beaked prows and purple moons painted along the hulls. Today, the last pithoi of olive oil, the last kegs of water and wine, the last foodstuffs of cheese and hard-crusted bread, raisins, dates, and dried figs, will be carried on board from the mule-drawn wagons sent by Aeacus. Tomorrow, if the gods send favorable winds, we will sail for the Isles of the Blest, a voyage of great distances and many perils, of dog-headed monsters with teeth as long as daggers and waves as tall as a three-storied palace. But Cretan ships can swim like dolphins, play in the troughs and mount the tallest wave. They have circumnavigated the great continent of Libya; I think they will find their way to our blessed islands.

Leaving my ship in the later afternoon, calling to Pandia as she painted the letters I-C-A-R-U-S below the prow, I have climbed for the last time to the cave which I call the Chamber of the Blue Monkeys, a forgotten shrine to the Great Mother. I have come to finish my history, written laboriously on papyrus and fastened together into a scroll like the famous Egyptian Book of the Dead. I shall leave the finished scroll in a copper chest for the Men of the future.

After we have sailed to the islands, I think that legend will not be kind to us. The Centaurs will thunder through many a battle as the barbarous foe of Men and their well-ordered cities; and the Minotaur, the Bull that Walks Like a Man, what will they say of him? His tail will grow forked, his horns will sprout like the antlers of a stag, and the gloom of his lightless caverns will terrorize children and young virgins. "Beast" will become synonymous with "animal," and "bestial" will be an epithet applied to savages and murderers. Men of the future, open this cave and find my scroll and read that we were neither gods nor demons, neither entirely virtuous nor entirely bad, but possessed of souls like you and in some ways kinder; capable of honor and sacrifice—and love. Consider if bestiality is not, after all, akin to humanity. Read and understand us, forgive us for having once defeated you, and forgive the author if he has allowed his own loss to darken his story.

I, Eunostos, Minotaur, thus conclude my history, the Passing of the Beasts.

EUNOSTOS,
MINOTAUR

* * * *

No sooner had I written the black, sprawling letters of my name than a hand touched my shoulder.

"Dearest Eunostos," she said. "I will not ask to read what you have written. If it is true, it has not drawn a pretty picture of me." A nimbus of light from the mouth of the cave illuminated her scarlet, belled skirt and the golden serpents around her wrists.

The nearness of her numbed me like a draught of wolf's-bane. At last I said: "Is it going well in Knossos? The Achaeans have not returned?"

"Not yet. One day, I think, they will surely conquer us. But not soon. We shall have a little more time in which to deserve a little more time."

"And Icarus is well?"

"He is a great hero. All the girls of Knossos are in love with him."

"And he with them?"

"With none of them."

"And you have come to tell me good-bye. It was kind of you, Thea."

"To tell you good-bye? My poor, foolish Minotaur, I have come to go with you, and not out of kindness either!"

"But the sea is treacherous," I cried. "Do you know the perils beyond the great pillars? The dog-headed monsters, the whirlpools, the clashing rocks—"

"It was I who chose your ships. The best in my father's fleet—at least, in what is left of his fleet."

"You will leave your father?"

"I have always loved him. But I came late to loving my mother. Now her people have called me."

I seized her hand and brought it reverently to my lips. "I will be your eternal friend!"

"Friend indeed! I will come as your wife or your woman, but not your friend. How shall we meet except through the flesh? The soul must see through the body's eyes and feed through the body's fingers, or else it is blind and unfeeling."

"You say that our bodies should meet. But you are beautiful—and I am a Beast."

"Yes, a Beast like my own mother, and lordlier than any Man I have every known! Do you know why I tried to eclipse you with clothes? Because you stirred me with feelings which had no place in my tidy garden of crocuses."

She removed the signet ring I had given her in the forest and laid it lovingly and yet with great finality beside my scroll. "This, my most loved possession, I shall leave for the Goddess and in memory of my friends, the blue monkeys. Having found my Minotaur, I can part with his ring."

With grave simplicity, she knelt at my feet. "Love has been a climbing for me, Eunostos. Now I have climbed until I can kneel to you."

"No, no," I pleaded. "You mustn't kneel!" I lifted her from the earth and held her in my arms, and she kissed me with such a sweet and burning ardor that she might have been one of the naughty Dryads who had studied the secrets of love for three hundred years. I held her with fierce tenderness and without shame and knew that love is not, as some poets say, a raging brush fire, but a hearthfire, which burns hotly, it is true, but in order to warm the cold sea-caves of the heart and light its pools with anemones of radiance.

"If only," I cried, "if only Icarus had come too!"

And of course he had, with Perdix.

Lightning Source UK Ltd.
Milton Keynes UK
UKOW04f0851260215

246890UK00002B/63/P